EVERYTHING FOR

everything for
BATHROOMS

INDEX

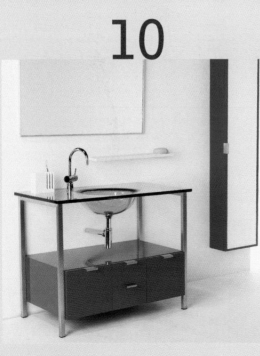

A bathroom. How many different things can be implied by a bathroom? Despite its immediate identification with merely hygienic and physiological functions, this space conceals significantly more complex connotations which are, on occasions, contradictory.

INTRODUCTION

In fact, they may be something different for each user, depending on a variety of conditioning factors. According to what each and every one of us may understand as hygiene. According to the love or hate relationship that every face maintains with its reflection. According to the idea that each body has of itself and of the care that it needs. According to the necessity that each spirit may have to withdraw from the exterior world. According to the capacity of each mind to find, in water, a source of indispensable energy and its ability to enjoy this discovery. According to each person's lifestyle and cultural background, because the bathroom in an apartment block in Manhattan is not the same as one found in a village of an African tribe, or one found in any working class district, or one belonging to a traditional Japanese family. It is not the same.

In this way, the bathroom, which such as it has existed for little more than a century, may be the best or the worst aspect of each home; a shelter or an area of transit; a temple of consecrated well-being to the regeneration of body and mind or a small dark unventilated room; a blank canvas on which our creativity can be liberated or a corner with a clinical and standardized appearance; a paradise for hedonistic spirits or an eminently functional space; a display of the latest technology or a river; a source of energy or mere procedure to enable the day to day to be confronted; a witness to experiences lived or evidence of the bitter passing of time; inspiration or expiration... and between these extremes, there is room for an infinite number of possibilities.

From the times in which having a bathroom inside the home became, particularly in areas of dense population, practically an obligation imposed by sanitary authorities as a means of preventing diseases produced by a lack of hygiene (at the beginning of the 20th century), this room has been subject to a spectacular evolution in the developments that have led to the currently predominant concepts of bathroom culture. As of the latter part of the 80's of the 20th century, after the innovations that were introduced into the kitchen, it was the bathroom's turn to be modernized. As a result, it has ceased to be situated in the smallest room of the house and to be ignored by architects, designers and manufacturers (who until then had felt it sufficient to produce standardized bathroomware and furniture) to become a space open to creativity and design in which, every day, we find innovations along with technical and aesthetic improvements destined to convert the ugly duckling of the home into a beautiful swan.

In this way, the bathroom becomes a place of inspiration, of renovation, of well being, of purification, it becomes a refuge from the stress of the city. In this way, man connects with his primitive roots, when water was considered to be a purifying element for body and soul that alleviated numerous diseases or prepared the devout for prayer and devotion. It is just that now, it is a place of preparation for day to day life. In fact, it is possible to trace the history of civilization by following the transformations that the bathroom has been subjected to over the years: from the old Roman hot baths, which were used collectively, to the present Jacuzzi, man and the architecture of domestic spaces have come a long way.

The new concept of bathrooms have converted this room into a place of intimacy, perhaps the only space within the home where it is possible to enjoy a few minutes of solitude and silence, where we can be alone directly in contact with our most authentic selves. The devices disappear and we see the reflection of our washed faces in the mirror, witness to our awakings, to our daily nature, our daily routine: 7:30 in the morning, wake up, shower, comb hair, brush teeth, put on lipstick, shave... the ritual of cleanliness, the ritual of life.

PATRICIA BUENO

BATHROOMWARE, FURNITURE AND ACCESSORIES

the new culture of wellbeing

In this century in which we have recently entered, the bathroom has managed to achieve the importance that it deserves and that, incomprehensibly, has been denied to it until now. In this new role, this space has become the ideal scene in which to integrate the re-discovered tradition of corporal regeneration, which belongs to antiquity, with the functional features necessary for hygiene, which belong to modernity, unifying, as a result, two ways of understanding the cleansing of the body that have been present throughout history.

This revision has led to the creation of a complete bathroom culture that has managed to free this space of its former boring and impersonal presence and convert it into a medium for the users to express their lifestyle. The times in which it was a mere functional space hidden away have come to an end. Now, its doors are fully opened, a better space is dedicated to it along with a larger budget, an entrance for natural light and ventilation are sought and its interiors are shown with pride.

The most well-known names from international design, such as Philippe Starck, Norman Foster, Matteo Thun, Antonio Citterio, Andrée Putman, Stefano Giovannoni, Michael Graves, Antonio Miró, Marcel Wanders or Claudio Silvestrin, among many, are working side by side with new talents and the most creative manufacturers of the sector to reinvent the bathroom. They are offering successive technical and aesthetic innovations that lead to an important evolution in the domestic environment with the principal aim being, as in all good design, the improvement of our society's lifestyle.

Because, let's see, whoever said that bathroomware had to be white and standardized, or that the furniture should be limited to a two-door cupboard and that the accessories should be of secondary importance? All of these preconceived ideas started to break down at the end of the 80's when a few pioneer companies started to see an excellent field for experimentation that presented an innumerable amount of technological and aesthetic challenges in this apparently monochromatic room. Since then, the bathroom has changed radically in appearance: the technological advances and new materials have enabled bathroomware, especially the washbasin, to take on any form or color imaginable and to become true exercises in ergonomics and aesthetics with and independent decorative value; as far as furniture is concerned, freedom is the word, from modular compositions to pieces that are almost sculptural in character, from glass to wood, from harmonizing groups to the most absolute contrasts, from minimalism to reminiscences of a rustic style, ...; the accessories, for their part, facilitate the tasks of daily cleanliness along with adding a touch of craziness or completing the group harmonically according to the tastes of each and every one of us. That is to say that the bathroom receives the treatment of a reborn saloon dedicated to wellbeing, a consecrated altar to the pleasure of our senses.

Bearing in mind the new tendencies impulsed by the present passion for the bathroom, amply represented in this chapter, what will the bathroom of the future be like? Perhaps, the major change will be that already foreseen for the bathroomware. The evolution of the bathroom is directly related to the way in which society evolves given that the change in the classical family structure (married couple with two or three children) has generated new ways of life and, consequently, new ways of using the home. This signifies that the bathroomware should achieve the same amount of flexibility currently offered by the furniture so as to be easily adaptable to the different lifestyles of its potential users. In this way, and by means of new systems of alimentation and drainage that permit the bathroomware to be installed and uninstalled quickly and easily, the bathroom will cease to be a fixed space and will become something mobile integrated into the home.

The objective is to achieve the maximum freedom when it comes to choice and nature so that each and every one of us can express exactly what it is that he or she understands as what a bathroom is and will be able to obtain exactly what he or she wishes for his or her space dedicated to his or her purification.

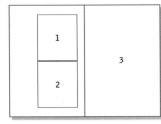

Photo page 11:
Washbasin "Allas Rectangular
IV" made in Durat®, a material developed by Tonester Ltd.
A solid material containing approximately 50% recycled and recyclable plastics. Available in 46 different colors.

1. Mirror with light from the collection "Light Modules" from Sieger
Design and Badkonzept Günter
Luther for Dornbracht.
2. Illumination wall from the collection "Light Modules" from Sieger
Design and Badkonzept Günter
Luther for Dornbracht.
3. Ceramic modules "Tatami" from
Ludovica and Roberto Palomba for
Flaminia.
These modules have been created as
architectural elements for the shower and can be arranged in many different ways. The textures on the ceramic elements have been developed
in such a way as to provide the benefits of a foot massage.

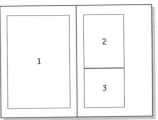

1. Wall containers from the "STARCK 1.2.3" collection and washbasin from the series "STARCK 1" designed by Philippe Starck for Duravit▪
This furnishing program stands out for its economy and versatility and for its combinations of wooden surfaces with frontal elements in plastics that incorporate high quality lacquered scratch-resistant finishes that are easy to clean▪

2. Furniture and sanitaryware from the series "CARO", design from Phoenix Product Design, and bathtub "DARO" in acrylic. All from Duravit▪

3. Container furniture from the "STARCK 1.2.3" collection and sanitaryware from the "STARCK 3" collection created by Philippe Starck for Duravit▪
The sanitaryware program "STARCK 3" is characterized by its square base form. Models especially designed for wheelchair accessibility are included in the program▪

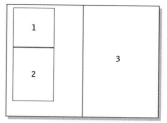

1. Ceiling light modules from the "LIGHT MODULES" collection from Sieger Design and Badkonzept Günter Luther for Dornbracht∎
This innovative and simple-to-assemble system allows for different types of lamps to be fitted on the modules∎
2. Cupboard "ALUMINIUM" from Jonathan Daifuku for Cosmic∎
Cupboard in anodized aluminum with sliding doors finished in a matt silver color. Available in a variety of sizes and finishes∎
3. Bathtub "KAOS" from the series "FLOYD" designed by Roberto and Ludovica Palomba. From Kos∎
Manufactured in acrylics over a steel structure. The faucets are the "TARA" model from Dornbracht∎

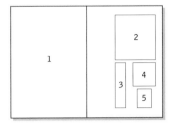

1. Shower system "PROXIMA". Design from Giovanni Ronzoni, Luisa Frigerio and Fabrizio Proserpio for Axolo▪ Both the shower base and column are in stainless steel while the sides are in 10-mm-thick transparent glass▪

2. Trolley from the "ISIDE" collection designed by Bruna Rapisarda for Pom D'Or▪ Manufactured in American oak with stainless steel base. Dimensions: 68 cm high × 47 cm wide × 35 long▪

3 and 4. Cupboard and container trolley from the series "CONTAINER". Design from Xavier Claramunt and Miguel De Mas for Cosmic▪ Container furniture made in wood veneered in light oak or American walnut. Available in various sizes▪

5. Box on wheels from the collection "FLUT02" designed by Stefano Spessotto for Cerasa▪ This box, contemplated for dirty clothes, forms part of an ample collection of furniture and sanitaryware▪

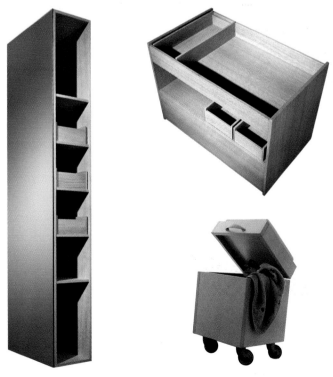

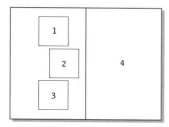

1 and 2. Mirrors "Daqva" and "Narciso" designed by Brunello Sighinolfi for Valli & Valli■
The model "Narciso" is formed by three superimposed mirrors and also includes a beauty-shaving mirror and halogen lamp■
3. Mirror "Alexis 3". Design from Studio Valli for Valli & Valli■
This model measures 80 cm in diameter■
4. Mirror "Eddy" from Marcello Ziliani and washbasin "Piu'" from Giancarlo Bartoli. All from Bertocci■
The mirror measures 65 cm in diameter and incorporates a light and a decorative element in frosted glass. The washbasin is available in three colors and four different versions■

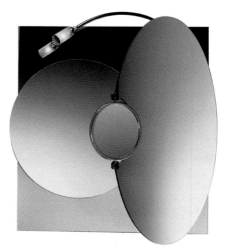

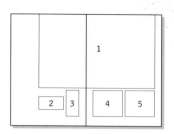

1. Washbasin and surface "XEN". Design from Marcus Sandler & Partners for Axolo▪
A balanced combination of materials in this composition with transparent glass basin, surface in wood and stainless steel support▪
2. Mirror "STRICT" from Michel Boucquillon for Valli & Valli▪
The dimensions of the mirror are 90 cm long × 40 cm wide▪
3. Mirror "OYA" from Michel Boucquillon for Valli & Valli▪
Beauty-shaving mirror incorporated. Dimensions: 103 cm high × 54.5 cm wide (including beauty-shaving mirror)▪
4 and 5. Wall beauty-shaving mirrors from the firm Samuel Heath▪

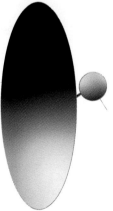

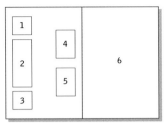

1. WC roll holder from the new Antonio Miro bathroom collection. Produced by Altro■
Support manufactured in chrome-plated brass and stainless steel with tube covered in natural cork■

2. Multiple towel rail produced by Samuel Heath■
Made in chrome-plated brass. Dimensions: 94 cm high × 61 cm wide■

3. Towel rail "Roy" from Valentina Downa for Valli & Valli■
Made in chrome-plated brass■

4. Mirror "Iside" designed by Bruna Rapisarda for Pom D'Or■
The frame is manufactured in American oak with wenge finish. Dimensions: 180 cm high × 60 cm wide■

5. Soap dish from the "Link" collection. Design from Angeletti & Ruzza for Colombo Design■

6. Composition "3002" formed by round stainless steel washbasins. A design from Lino Codato for the firm Axia■

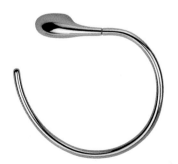

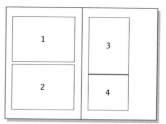

Previos pages:
Bathtub "LADY-X" in stainless steel designed by Giovanni Ronzoni, Luisa Frigerio and Fabrizio Proserpio for the firm Axolo■

1. Bathtub "TAUS LINE" from System-Pool (Grupo Porcelanosa)■
2. Bathtub and washbasin "GOBI". Design from Marcel Wanders with mirrors "SQUARE" from Piero Lissoni. From Boffi■
Bathtub and washbasin made in a new material, *Cristal Plant*. The bathtub incorporates the faucet "MINIMAL" designed by Giulio Gianturco■
3. Washbasin and accessories from the series "PLATE". Design from Giancarlo Vegni for Bertocci■
Manufactured in stainless steel and glass■
4. Sanitaryware "KONO" that belongs to the "PROYECTO HERA" collection designed by Sabrina Selli for Althea Ceramica■
Innovative toilet and bidet with conical forms and steel bases■

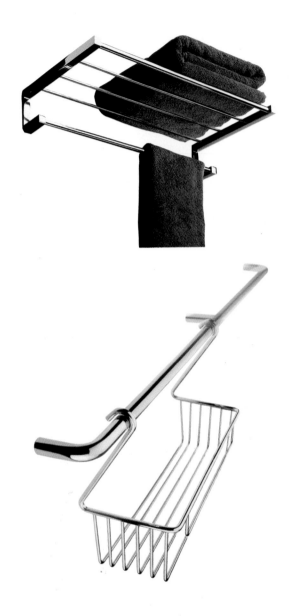

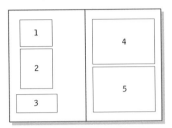

1. Towel shelf from the "METRIC" collection from Pom D'Or■ Dimensions: 60 cm wide × 30 cm deep■

2. Hanging container from the "WORKING" collection. Design from Roger Ferrer, Miguel Ordiales and Mónica Gonzalez for Cosmic■ Made in brass and available in a chrome or matt chrome finish■

3. Towel shelf from Samuel Heath■ Made in chrome-plated brass■

4. Freestanding bathtub from the series "EDITION PUTMAN" created by the French designer Andrée Putman for Hoesch■

5. Freestanding bathtub "MEGAFORM OVALADA" from Kaldewei■ The bathtub is manufactured in Starylan® or enameled steel Kaldewei®■

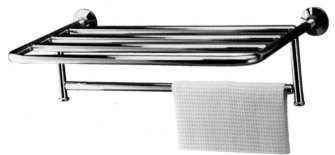

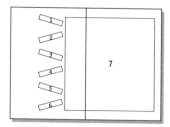

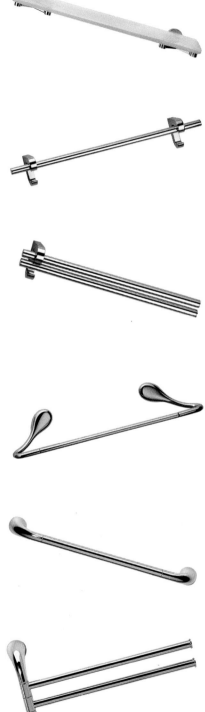

1. Rack "SPLASH" designed by Sottsass Associati (Ettore Sottsass and Christopher Redform) for Valli & Valli■
Manufactured in matt metacrylate. Dimensions: 54.5 cm long × 13.8 cm wide■

2 and 3. Towel rails from the series "PONCTUATION" created by Andrée Putman for Valli & Valli■
Manufactured in chrome-plated brass■

4. Towel rail "LACCIOLO" design from Piano Design for Valli & Valli■
Manufactured in chrome-plated brass■

5 and 6. Towel rails for one or two towels from the "SOFT" collection. Design from Paolo Pedrizzetti for Valli & Valli■

7. Freestanding bathtub from the series "EDITION PUTMAN" developed by Andrée Putman for Hoesch■
The original aluminum covering contrasts with the acrylic material used in the inside and rack in solid wood■

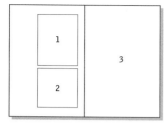

1. Washbasin "FUORI" designed by Carlo Urbinati for Art Ceram■ .
2. Tabletop accessories from the collection "KYOTO". Design from Studiopoco for Gedy■
Accessories with ceramic interiors and wooden outer casings■
3. Sanitaryware from the series "ARCADIA SUSPENDIDO" from Bellavista■

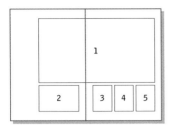

1. Furniture collection for the bathroom "Iside". Design from Bruna
Rapisarda for Pom D'Or■
Furniture made in American oak
with finishes in wenge and white ceramic washbasins (these are also
manufactured in stainless steel)■
2. Benches for the bathroom from
the series "Zen" from Toscoquattro■
3. Porcelain accessories from the
"Jamila" collection. Design from
Studiopoco for Gedy■
4. Accessories from the "Strict"
collection designed by Michel Boucquillon for Valli & Valli■
5. Tabletop accessories from the series "Letizie Flash" from OML■
Manufactured in chrome-plated brass
and polyester resin■

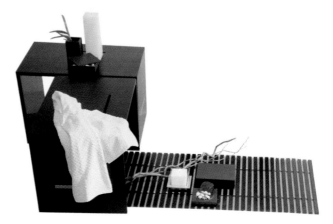

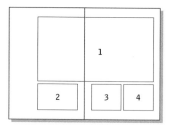

Previos pages:
Bathroom made up with pieces from the series "I FIUMI". Design from Claudio Silvestrin for Boffi.
The washbasin "ADIGE" and the bathtub "PO" are made in stone.

1. Composition from the "FENG-SHUI" collection from Toscoquattro.
2. Washbasin "CARRE'" from Bertocci. Square-shaped washbasin made in transparent glass with stainless steel support.
3. A piece from the series "HABANA" from Sanico.
Consists of glass top, four-drawer cabinet made in MDF lacquered in a brilliant finish and polished by hand and stainless steel legs.
4. Composition from the series "NEO" from Sanico.
The one-piece washbasin is manufactured in resin (Stonefeel) and is a design from Nacho Lavernia and Alberto Cienfuegos. The top and drawer set on castors are manufactured in MDF lacquered in a brilliant finish and polished by hand.

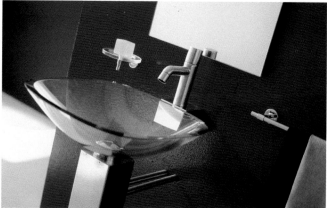

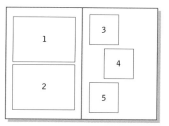

1 and 2. Two possible compositions from the modular furniture collection "PLUVIA" from Toscoquattro■

3. Washbasin with vanity top "WATERPROOF" designed by Roger Ferrer, Miguel Ordiales and Mónica Gonzalez for Cosmic■
Made in an innovative material: aluminum hydroxide with synthetic resin. Available in various sizes■

4. Washbasin "ACQUAGRANDE" with towel rail. Design from Giulio Cappellini and Ludovica Palomba. From Flaminia■
Made in porcelain with an anthracite finish■

5. Washbasin from the series "LIQUID". Design from Nuria Coll and Willi Kunzel for Cosmic■
Made with aluminum hydroxide with synthetic resin. An original drainage system has been incorporated■

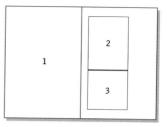

1. Composition proposed by Flaminia■

The washbasin is the model "ACQUA-GRANDE". Design from Giulio Cappellini and Ludovica Palomba. The vanity top and cabinet are manufactured in dark oak wood and are a design from Roberto and Ludovica Palomba as is the mirror "LINE". The vitrified mosaic is from Bisazza■

2. Washbasin "TWIN SET" with "TWIN COLUMN" stand. Design from Roberto and Ludovica Palomba for Flaminia■

The faucet is a design from Sieger Design for Dornbracht■

3. Washbasin from the program "OPEN SPACE" from Ceramica Globo■

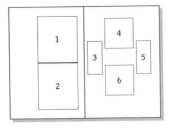

1. Washbasins "On" integrated in the Proyecto Hera developed by Sabrina Selli for Althea Ceramica▪
2. Washbasin and furniture from the program "Open" from Sanico▪
The washbasin is in white porcelain and the various cabinets combine wenge with aluminum and chrome-plated brass▪
3, 4, 5 and 6. Accessories from the "City" collection. Designs by Nacho Lavernia and Alberto Cienfuegos for Sanico▪
This collection of accessories combine chrome-plated brass with a matt white resin (Stonefeel). Delta de Plata Prize ADI-FAD 2003▪

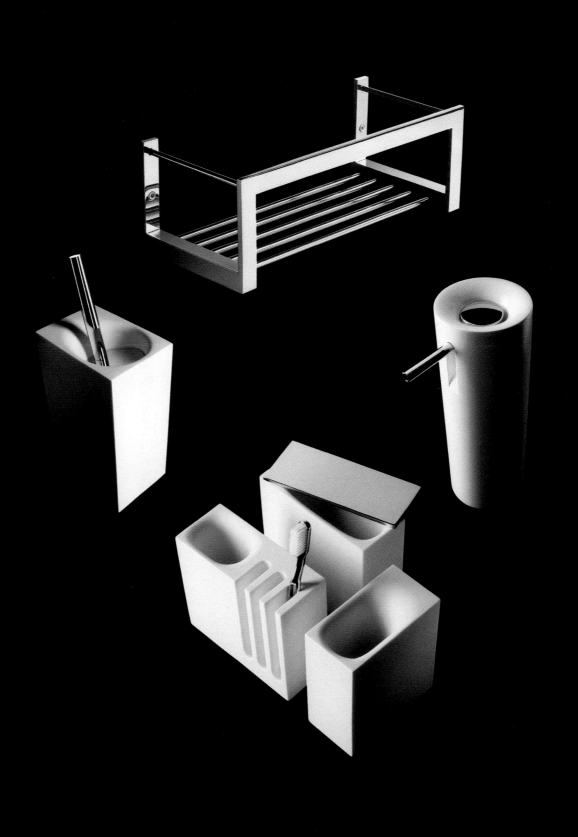

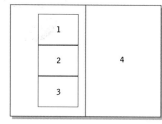

1, 2 and 3. Washbasin "LIGHT LTB"
and bathtub "LIGHT LTT". Designs
by Jan Puylaert for Wet■
This revolutionary sanitaryware is
manufactured in 100% recyclable
polyethylene and can be easily installed wherever desired. The incorporated illumination has been developed by means of an LED system
that has been produced in collaboration with the company CheckUp.
It is programmed to illuminate in
more than 1,250 colors. Prize for
innovation, Design Plus 2003■
4. Washbasins "QUADROTTO". Design
from Bruna Rapisarda for Regia■
Manufactured in glass-resin■

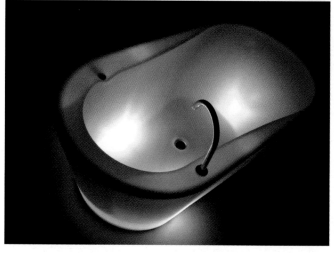

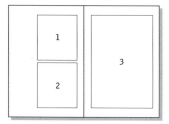

1 and 2. Cabinet and shelf with light from the collection "META PLASMA" created by Sieger Design for Dornbracht▪

Furniture manufactured in intense colors in a special reflective transparent synthetic material that makes the edges of every object glow depending on how they catch the light▪

3. Toilet from the series "STARCK 3" created by Philippe Starck for Duravit▪

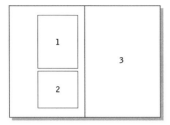

| 1 | 3 |
| 2 | |

1. Collection of accessories "MALIBU" created by Itamar Harari for Gedy▪ Manufactured in thermoplastic resin and available in various colors▪

2. Accessories from the collection "LETIZIE DARDO". Design from Studio Cibò for OML▪

These articles combine chrome-plated brass with colored polycarbonate▪

3. Washbasin "WT.MC" from Alape▪ This piece has the peculiarity of being manufactured in verified steel, a material with a reduced weight that enables the washbasin to be fitted on to the wall. It offers a large vanity top▪

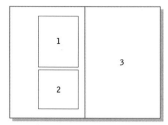

Previos pages:
One of the possible arrangements of the complete program "IL BAGNO ALESSI" developed by Stefano Giovannoni for Alessi∎
The program includes porcelain pieces and sanitaryware manufactured by Laufen, faucets manufactured by Oras and furniture, accessories and shower cubicles manufactured by Inda∎

1. Accessories from the series "SEVENTY" designed by Matteo Thun for Gedy∎
Manufactured in thermoplastic resin and available in various colors∎
2. Wall brush holder from the series "YOGA". Design from Francesco Lucchese for Colombo Design∎
3. Collection of sanitaryware "SENSE" from Permesso viewed from above∎

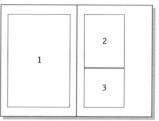

1. Composition with the model "Zᴇɴɪᴛ" from Cerasa■
Modular project that allows for numerous arrangements. The surfaces and drawers are in MDF lacquered with a brilliant finish and the handles and legs are in matt aluminum■

2 and 3. Washbasin from the series "Sᴛᴀʀᴄᴋ 2" and bathtub "Sᴛᴀʀᴄᴋ" designed by Philippe Starck for Duravit■
The washbasin measures 4.5 cm in width and the bathtub 180 cm in length × 80 cm in width■

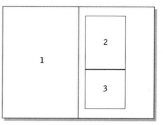

1. Sanitaryware collection "YOU & ME" from Hatria

2. Accessories "EQUIS". Design from Nacho Lavernia and Alberto Cienfuegos for Sanico

Made in white porcelain and stainless steel

3. Washbasin "ZENIT" from Cerasa

Manufactured in colored metacrylate and available in red, yellow, blue, opal and white with matt aluminum stand with incorporated towel rail

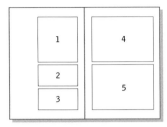

1. Mirror "CHANGE" designed by James Irvine for Duravit.
This mirror supposes an authentic novelty by incorporating regulable lighting units that change the mood of the bathroom.
2. Wall lamp "DOLLY". Design from Nacho Lavernia and Alberto Cienfuegos for Sanico.
Made in aluminum and glass triplex opal in various lengths.
3. Wall lamp "ALBA". Design from Nacho Lavernia and Alberto Cienfuegos for Sanico.
This metal wall lamp can be fitted in a horizontal or vertical position.
4. Sanitaryware from the Proyecto Hera developed by Sabrina Selli for Cerámica Althea.
The washbasin is the model "CORNER" with incorporated towel rail.
5. Sanitaryware from the program "SENSE" from the firm Permesso.

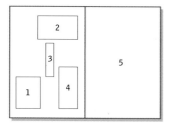

1. Brush rack "PENCIL". Design from Mauro Artusio for Gedy. Manufactured in thermoplastic resin.
2. Top "MR. SUICIDE". Design from Massimo Giacon for Alessi.
3. Brush rack "TOQ". Design from Platt & Young for Koziol.
4. Dirty clothes basket "CRAZY COW" form Outlook Zelco.
5. Plunger "JOHNNY THE DIVER" created by Stefano Giovannoni for Alessi.

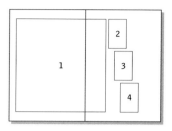

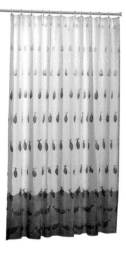

1. Vanity unit that integrates wash-basin and glass surface. It is the model "Bignè" from Tulli Zuccari.
2. Shower curtain "Bypass". Design from Silvia Buso for Gedy.
Made in polyester.
3. Shower curtain "Waterfall". Design from Clara Grassi for Gedy.
Made in PVC.
4. Shower curtain "Planets". Design from Carol Lanza for Gedy.
Made in polyester.

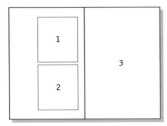

1. Chrome stool from the series "Kubic" from Bruna Rapisarda for Pom D'Or.
Dimensions: 40 cm high × 20 cm in diameter.
2. Stool "Sit" created by Bartoli Design for Colombo Design.
3. Bench "Think Bank" designed by Fréderic Dedelley for the new "Interiors" collection from Dornbracht.
Folding bench manufactured in solid iroko wood and stainless steel. Dimensions: 140 cm in length × 39.5 cm in height × 52.5 cm in width.

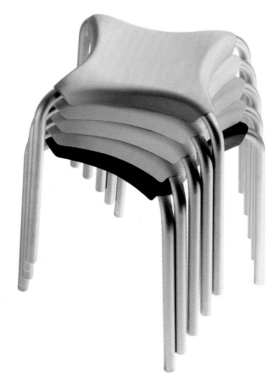

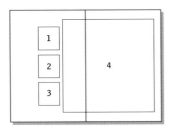

1, 2 and 3. Bathroom scales "GREEN", "SUMMER" and "GRAND PRIX" from Outlook Zelco■
4. Composition with a light rustic air from the series "COTTA" from Keramag■

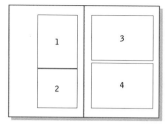

1. Bathroom furniture and wash-basin from the collection "FRONTAL" from Struch▪

The furniture is finished in genuine wood veneer in a light cherry tone. The width of this composition is 100 cm▪

2. The modular furniture line "CAL-ICO'". Design from Marconato and Zappa for Altamarea▪

Available in four different finishes and with a variety of washbasins in terms of materials and sizes▪

3. Bathroom furniture from the series "OAK" with one-piece top and surface in glass from Q'In▪

4. Group of furniture from the series "ALOE" from the collection Bellavista Concept from Bellavista▪

Consists of surface with fitted circular washbasins, low shelf and glass-fronted cabinet, drawer and small cupboard. Available finished in cherry or wenge▪

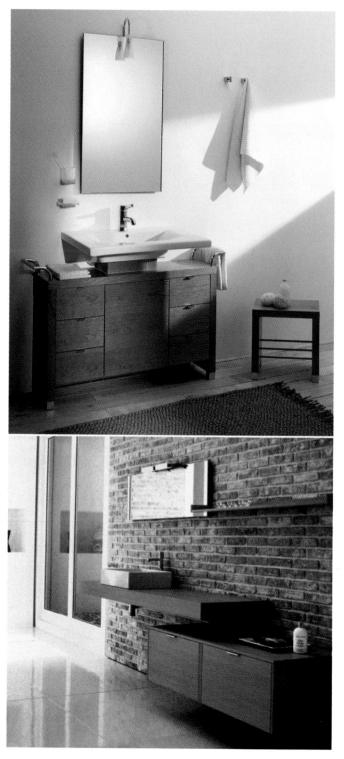

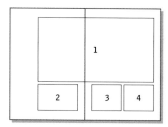

1. Bathroom made up of elements from the "AERI" collection from Altro■
Washbasin made in seven-mm-thick wood by means of innovative curving and wood gluing techniques. The collection has received the Design Plus 2003 Prize awarded by the ISH - Frankfurt Trade Fair■
2. Washbasin "QUATTRO" from the collection Bellavista Concept from Bellavista■
3. One-piece washbasin "CITY". Design from Nacho Lavernia and Alberto Cienfuegos for Sanico■
It is manufactured in marble or resin (Stonefeel)■
4. Washbasin from the new integral collection of bathroom services Antonio Miro Bathroom. Produced by Altro■
The washbasin in black porcelain is inserted into a solid iroko wood module that has been hand-treated with special oils■

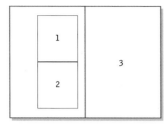

1. Mirror "HOT/COLD" designed by Roberto and Ludovica Palomba for Flaminia∎
Dimensions: 100 cm in height × 42 cm in width. The towel rail is the model "HOP" designed by King and Roselli. The faucet is from the firm Dornbracht and the mosaic is from Bisazza∎
2. Wall WC roll holder and brush holder "HOP" from King and Roselli for Flaminia∎
The wall hung toilet and bidet are examples of the "SPIN" model. Design from Roberto and Ludovica Palomba∎
3. Composition made up using elements from the "BÁSICO" collection from Gama-Decor∎
Complete modular program consisting of washbasins, accessories and furniture manufactured in different finishes and materials∎

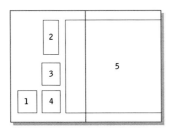

1. Liquid soap dispenser "KEKO JDT" from Vieler International▪ Made in glass and stainless steel▪
2. Original WC roll holder "CLOJO" designed by Henk Stallinga for the firm Stallinga▪
3. Hanger from the series "STUDIO" from Smedbo▪ Made in chrome-plated brass▪
4. Towel rail from the series "LOFT" from Smedbo▪ Made in chrome-plated brass with matt finish▪
5. Composition from the collection "BÁSICO" from Gama-Decor▪ The modules are available in a great diversity of formats and finishes so that completely personalized compositions can be created that match other elements from this bathroom program▪

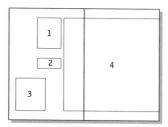

Previos pages:
Composition formed by sanitaryware and container modules from the "OPEN SPACE" collection from Cerámica Globo■

1. Accessories from the series "ISIDE". Design from Bruna Rapisarda for Pom D'Or■
Made in American oak■
2. Wall soap dish from the series "ISIDE". Design from Bruna Rapisarda for Pom D'Or■
3. Container with castors and waste bin "TANGO" from Sanico■
Veneered in natural cherry, sycamore or American walnut■
4. Compositions from the complete bathroomware program "IL BAGNO ALESSI" developed by Stefano Giovannoni for Alessi■
The program includes sanitaryware manufactured by Laufen, faucets manufactured by Oras and furniture, accessories and shower cubicles manufactured by Inda■

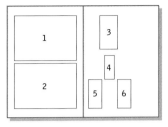

1. Composition from the collection "AERI" from Altro■

All of the elements are made in stainless steel and aluminum. The washbasin in three-mm-thick stainless steel has been sand blasted to achieve a matt finish■

2. Washbasin "DUE" integrated in the Proyecto Hera developed by Sabrina Selli for Cerámica Althea■

This washbasin is presented hung on the wall or on either of two supports made in stainless steel or wood. It incorporates a towel rail and spacious surface■

3. Mirror with incorporated clock "INTIME" created by Claudio La Viola for Nito■

4. Tabletop beauty-shaving mirror from the collection "FRONTAL" from Struch■

5. Mirror "VENEZIA" designed by Tommaso Gagliardi for Nito■

6. Mirror "WISH" with glass frame from Dafne Koz for Nito■

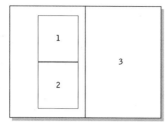

1. Self-carrying washbasin "TóTEM" de Damián Sánchez for Artquitect Edition■
Washbasin in the form of a rectangular prism with intense black granite base and white marble interior. It measures 85 cm in height. It is complemented with the accessories "CONTINUA". ■

2. Washbasin "KONO". Part of the Proyecto Hera from de Sabrina Selli for Cerámica Althea■
Ceramic washbasin in a conical form with steel structure■

3. Washbasin "STANDARD" from Vitraform■
Oval washbasin manufactured in ten-mm-thick laminated glass by means of an exclusive process. Available in different colors and finishes■

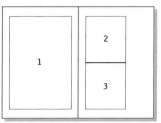

1. Washbasin "Box" designed by Jeffrey Bernett and faucet "CUT" from Mario Tessarollo and Tiberio Cerato. Produced by Boffi■

The cavity of the washbasin is made in Ekotek (composed resin) and offers a practical storage surface below. The faucet is in stainless steel and holds three different patents: one for the design, another for the function and one for the mechanisms■

2. Mirror "CHANGE" and modular container furniture "IN THE MOOD". Design from James Irvine for Duravit■

3. Double washbasin "DOPPIO VEDO". Design from Stefano Bertocci for Bertocci■

It is manufactured in transparent, frosted or blue glass■

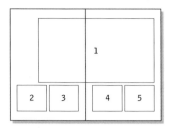

1. Bathroom range "QUADRATA" easily identified due to its rectilinear lines. From System-Pool■

2. Washbasin "SPOON" designed by Nacho Lavernia and Alberto Cienfuegos for Sanico■
Manufactured in white porcelain with a large vanity top■

3. Washbasin "FUORI SCALA QUADRO" designed by Carlo Urbinati for Art Ceram■

4. Washbasin and support "MOON" from Sanico■
The washbasin has been hewn out of solid stone, the top finished with a natural wood veneer and the support is in chrome-plated steel■

5. Washbasin "FREESTANDING" with vanity top from Vitraform■
Both washbasin and vanity top are manufactured in ten-mm-thick laminated glass. Ten different colors can be chosen from■

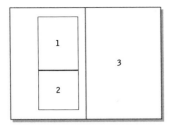

1. Cabinet "Big Pill". Design from Roberto and Ludovica Palomba for Dornbracht∎
Rounded hung cabinet made in MDF and lacquered in white. Measures 42 cm in diameter∎
2. Dispenser for makeup cleansing discs "Up-Pill" designed by Stefano Giovannoni for Alessi∎
3. Brush and soap holder "Gustav". Design from Mauro Artusio for Gedy∎ Manufactured in Surlyn® (registered trade name belonging to DuPont®)∎

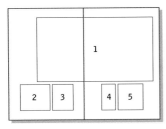

1. Wall hung washbasin in white porcelain from the "You & Me" collection from Hatria◾

2. Nail clippers "Canaglia". Design from Stefano Pirovano for Alessi◾

3. Brush holders "Dr. Kiss" from Philippe Starck for Alessi◾

4. Wall clock with suction pad "Ben" from Koziol◾
Measurements: 16 cm in height × 10 cm in width◾

5. Wall magazine holder with suction pad "Bahia Gi" from Outlook Zelco◾

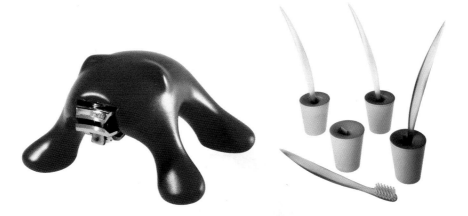

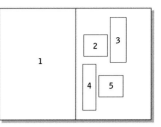

1. Multifunctional bathroom column "SOLITUDE" from Dornbracht■
This column integrates the areas of shower and general cleanliness by the incorporation of numerous additional features such as the thermostat module xTOOL and the basin faucet Tara■

2. Sponge shelf in steel from the collection of accessories "FRONTAL" from Struch■

3. Accessory from the collection "FRONTAL" from Struch■
Incorporates two movable towel rails, two acrylic trays and a liquid soap dispenser■

4. Bathroom cupboard from the series "LIQUID". Design from Núria Coll and Willi Kunzel for Cosmic■
Made by sandwiching anodized aluminum and aluminum hydroxide with synthetic resin. Measurements: 100 cm in height × 25 cm in width■

5. Shelf with container tray "TECHNO". Design from Roger Ferrer, Miguel Ordiales and Mónica González for Cosmic■
Made in brushed stainless steel AISI-316■

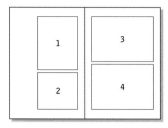

1. Washbasin with stand sheathed in steel from the program "OPEN SPACE" from Ceramica Globo▪
2. Washbasin "BOX" from Bruna Rapisarda for Regia▪
The cavity of the washbasin and support are in stainless steel while the vanity top is in transparent glass▪
3. Bathroom furniture from the collection "CLIO" de Milldue▪
4. Composition from the model "MODERN TILE" from Cerasa▪
This model consists of structures manufactured with panels constructed in water-repellant materials contemplated to facilitate the distribution of the bathroom. They are combined with fronts, doors, glass cases and drawers in MDF that are lacquered in a wide range of colors▪

1. Composition proposed by Boffi▪
The bathtub is the model "GOBI", design from Marcel Wanders, accompanied by the faucet "MINIMAL" from Giulio Gianturco. The handbasin is the model "BOX", design from Jeffrey Bernett, accompanied by the faucet "CUT", design from Tessarollo and Cerato. The mirror "TOOLS" is a design from Piero Lissoni and the lamp "LUMI" is a creation from Klaesson, Koivisto and Rune▪

2. Bathtub from the series "500". Design from Antonio Citterio with Sergio Brioschi for Pozzi-Ginori (Grupo Sanitec)▪

3. Built-in Bathtub designed by the architect Norman Foster for Hoesch▪ A design that proposes a contemporary interpretation of the classic zinc tub. It is manufactured in four sizes and allows for the installation of a hydromassage system▪

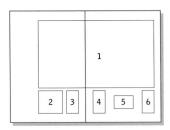

1. Bathroom range "Redondata". Designed and produced by System-Pool (Grupo Porcelanosa)■
2. Dental floss dispenser "Kai P". Idea from Nora Dold and developed by the firm Koziol■
3. Makeup cleansing disc dispenser "Florence" designed by Seventh Sense and Koziol■
Measurements: 19.9 cm in height × 8.2 cm in width × 8.2 cm in length■
4. Wall dispenser from the collection "Frontal" from Struch■
5. Wall soap dish from the series of bathroom accessories from Axor (Hansgrohe)■
6. Liquid soap dispenser from the collection "Iside" from Bruna Rapisarda for Pom D'Or■

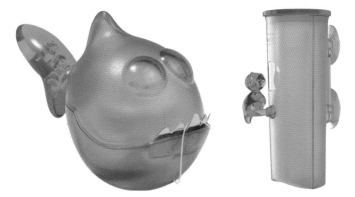

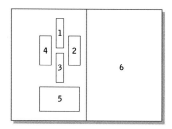

1. Brush holder "Sheeva". Design from Davide Vercelli and Andrea Cerminara for Ritmonio▪

2. WC roll holder with reserve "Gilbert". Design from Henk Stallinga for Stallinga▪

3. Floor brush holder from the collection "Frontal" from Struch▪
Manufactured with an extractable acrylic interior recipient▪

4. Brush holder from the accessory collection "Outline" from Smedbo▪

5. Collection of brush holders from the series "Frac" designed by Cinzia Ruggeri for Nito▪
Made up of ten different models with chrome-plated brass bases and decorative colored glass terminations▪

6. Wall hung toilet and bidet from the collection "Link". Design from Giulio Cappellini and Roberto and Ludovica Palomba for Flaminia. The faucet is from Dornbracht▪

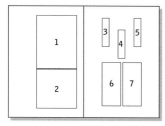

1. WC roll holder "Antonio C" from Guido Venturini for Alessi■

2. Brush holder "Merdolino" from Stefano Giovannoni for Alessi■

3. Brush holder "Filoforte" from Maurizio Duranti for Valli & Valli■ Made in Chrome-plated brass■

4. Brush holder from the collection "G-32-F" from Pom D'Or■

5. Brush holder from the series "Frame". Design from Massimiliano della Monaca and Davide Vercelli for Ritmonio■

6. Double WC roll holder and free-standing brush holder model "Kubic" from Pom D'Or■
A magazine rack is also included. Made in stainless steel. Measurements: 61 cm high × 28 cm wide × 25 cm long■

7. Wall column from the series "Isole". Design from Anna and Carlo Bartoli for Colombo Design■
Includes, in a minimum of space, brush and holder, WC roll holder, towel rail and soap dish. Made in chrome-plated brass and acid treated glass■

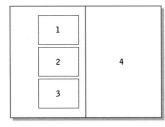

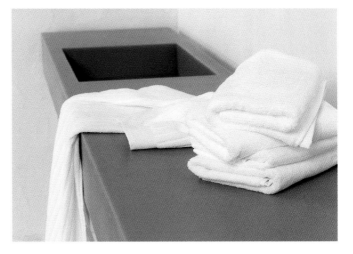

1. Washbasin and vanity top "ALLAS RECTANGULAR WM IV" made in one piece of Durat®, material developed by the company Tonester Ltd.
Manufactured in Durat®, a new composite material containing approximately 50% recycled and completely recyclable plastics. Available in 46 colors.
2.
2. Bathtub "BLOCK" designed by M. Claesson, E. Koivisto and O. Rune for Durat® (produced by Tonester Ltd).
One of the characteristics of this new material, Durat®, is its warm and silky touch and the impression of depth that is given by its special finish.
3. Marble washbasin for the vanity top "DUOMO" from L'Antic Colonial.
Measurements: 55 cm in width × 48 cm in length × 9 cm in height.
4. Acrylic bathtub from the series "FLOYD". Design from Roberto and Ludovica Palomba for Kos.
The faucet is from Dornbracht.

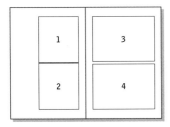

1. Glass washbasin "FREESTANDING" with the fitting system "MONO MOUNT" from Vitraform■
The washbasin is manufactured in ten-mm-thick laminated glass and is available in 12 different colors■
2. Washbasin "FREESTANDING" with white glass vanity top. From Vitraform■
This model is presented with fine lines etched in the glass. Both washbasin and vanity top are manufactured in 10-mm-thick laminated glass■
3. Composition from the series "ALKIMIA" from Cerasa■
Modular series with fronts in MDF lacquered or with varnished oak veneer. The washbasin is manufactured in marble resin■
4. Environment composed of sanitaryware and accessories designed by Philippe Starck for Duravit and Axor (Hansgrohe)■
The sanitaryware is produced by Duravit, the faucet is from Axor and the accessories are from Duravit and Axor■

Previous pages:
Composition with minimalist aesthetics using elements designed by Giulio Cappellini and Roberto and Ludovica Palomba for Flaminia.
The washbasin is the model "Acqua-grande", the vanity top, in solid oak, is the model "Brick" and the ceramic modules placed in the shower base are from the "Tatami" model.

1. Container furniture "Lay-Up", design from Studio Saba, and bathtub "Lavasca Mini" from Matteo Thun. All from Rapsel.
The small containers are manufactured in colored glass and are stackable. The bathtub is manufactured in a mineral composite called cristalplant.
2. Wall medicine chest "Ermes" from Giovanna Talocci for Nito. Manufactured in Duralmond, a material obtained from almond shells.
3. Bathtub "Carezza Lake", from de Peter Büchele, and shower "Cobra", from Adri Hazebröek. All from Rapsel.
The bathtub is manufactured in stainless steel. The exterior has a brushed finish while the interior has been polished. The shower with incorporated siphon and mixer is in brushed stainless steel.

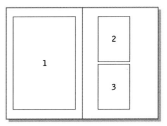

1. Soap dishes from the series "BLACK". Design from Sara Mano for PnP▪
Produced in plastic and available in five different colors▪

2. Shower system "BOX BAMBOLO" and ceramic flooring "TATAMI" designed by Roberto and Ludovica Palomba for Flaminia▪
Shower measurements: 210 cm in height × 90 cm in width × 90 cm in length▪

3. Freestanding mirror with castors "TURN AROUND" designed by Rodolfo Dordoni for the collection Interiors from Dornbracht▪
Made with a steel frame and holds three acrylic trays. Measurements: 180 cm in height × 45 cm in width × 40 cm in depth▪

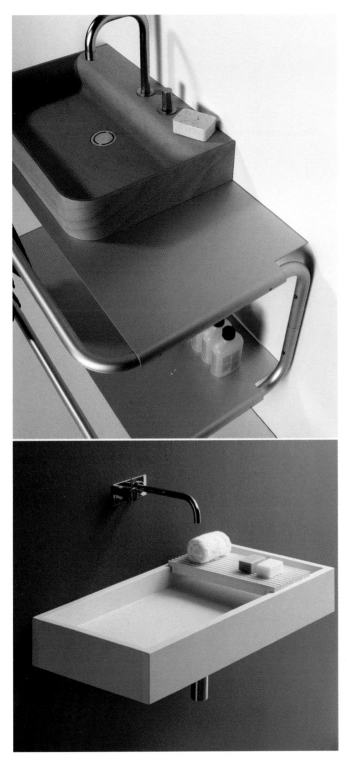

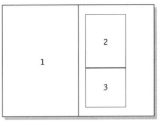

1. Bathroom program "Midi" from Francesc Rifé. Produced by MB and Artquitect Edition▪
Bathroom furnishing system made with aluminum trimmings and solid metacrylate fronts. The handbasin is manufactured in a mineral and resin composite▪
2. Washbasin and vanity top from the collection "Aeri" from Altro▪
The washbasin is manufactured in curved seven-mm-thick wood and the vanity unit is in aluminum. Prize-winner of the Design Plus 2003 Prize awarded by the ISH - Frankfurt Trade Fair▪
3. Washbasin from the collection "Barcelona" from Matteo Thun for Rapsel▪
The washbasins from this collection stand out for their invisible drainage system. They are manufactured in various materials, sizes and finishes▪

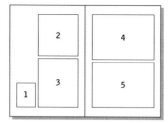

1. Cupboard "Poppy" from Studio Decoma for Valli & Valli▪

Made in anodized aluminum with eight adjustable shelves the cupboard is available in three different heights: 168 cm, 107 cm or 86 cm▪

2. Wall brush holder from the collection "Viva" from Bartoli Design for Colombo Design▪

3. Washbasin "Betty Blue" from Alape▪

This special design stands out for its original drainage system▪

4. Washbasin "Mohave" and auxiliary unit from Roca▪

The washbasin is made in porcelain and the furniture in natural wood with a wenge finish▪

5. Asymmetric washbasin from the collection "Easy". Design from Antonio Citterio with Sergio Brioschi for Pozzi-Ginori (Grupo Sanitec)▪

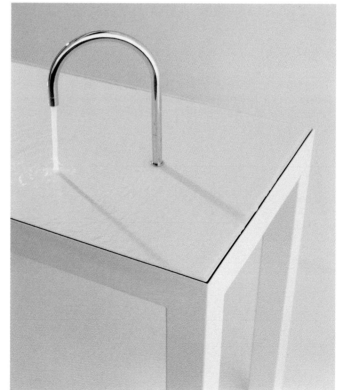

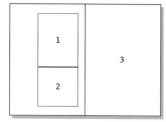

1. Double handbasin "DUETTO". Design from Claudio Brambilla for Nito■
Made in ceramic. Its length of 130 cm indicates a technical success for the ceramic industry■
2. Furniture collection "POP" from Stefano Cavazzana for Nito■
Made in plywood■
3. Handbasin "BLOC" from José Luis López Ibáñez for Artquitect Edition■
Square basin made in high-temperature porcelain in various colors or in gray and beige natural sandstone. The side measurement is 50 cm■

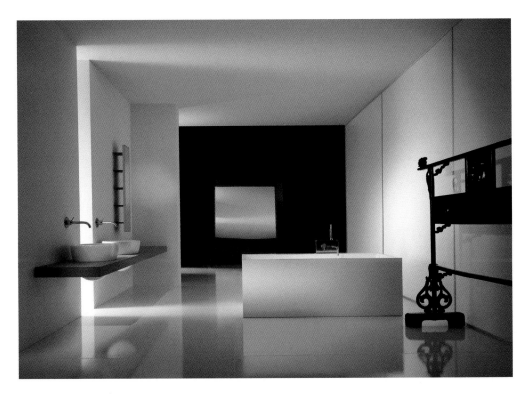

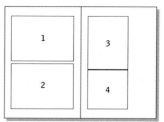

1. Composition proposed by the firm Boffi■

Stone washbasin "ADIGE" from the series I Fiumi designed by Claudio Silvestrin; washbasin tap "DISKO" from KWC; bathtub "MOOD" from Claesson, Koivisto and Rune; Mirror "TOOLS" from Piero Lissoni■

2. Freestanding bathtub "FREE BY BABEL" designed by Adolf Babel for Hoesch■

The shell of the tub is composed of translucent sanitary acrylic, which requires no reinforcement, and stands on a noble wooden platform and is framed by four columns that are also made of wood. A hydromassage system can also be incorporated■

3. Bathtub "AVVENTURA" designed by Adolf Babel for Hoesch■

Bathtub characterized by its unusual depth of 570 mm. Also available with an incorporated hydromassage system■

4. Bathtub shelf "CROSS OVER SET". Design from Torsten Neeland for the collection Interiors from Dornbracht■ Made in anodized aluminum with glass pearls. A mirror and a system to hold books are also incorporated■

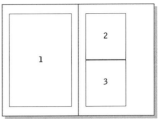

1. Bathtub "STARCK" and container with castors from the furniture program for economic bathrooms "STARCK 1.2.3". Design from Philippe Starck for Duravit▪

2. Shower cubicle "IMA" from Peter Büchele for Rapsel▪
This system allows a shower cubicle to be created in the bathtub that opens and closes like a book. It is fitted to the wall and manufactured with a structure in stainless steel and panels in water-resistant fabric▪

3. Shower cubicle "MIMI" from Peter Büchele for Rapsel▪
Made with a stainless steel structure and transparent tempered glass panels. The wall washbasin in glass and stainless steel is the model "HOMAGE A SHEILA" designed by Studio Rapsel and Gianluigi Landoni▪

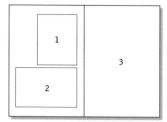

1. Washbasin with integrated stand "WT.RX" from Alape.
Made in enameled steel.
2. Washbasin "NUDA", auxiliary furniture in light oak and mirror from the collection "SIMPLE" designed by Roberto and Ludovica Palomba for Flaminia.
3. Shower system "PLUVIA", design from Matteo Thun, with teak base "PIANOLEGNO", design from Berger & Sthal. All from Rapsel.
The base in wood measures 84 cm × 30 cm.

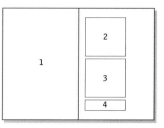

1. Sanitaryware from the collection "Arq. Collection" from Gala∎
This collection is made up of sanitaryware, bathroom furniture, bathtubs and shower bases. The sanitaryware is made in sanitary porcelain∎
2. Washbasin from the "Sistema Verso" from Ceramica Catalano∎
Original rectangular washbasin with unusual measurements: 50 cm long × 25 cm wide. The wall hung toilet and bidet are from the "Sistema Zero"∎
3. Composition made up of elements with rounded forms from the collection "Calm" from Permesso∎
4. Collection of hand bowls and basins "Discus" from Joan Raventós for Artquitect∎
Manufactured in ceramics following traditional methods, they are hand turned and glazed, which means that no two are exactly alike. Available in 15 colors∎

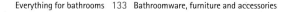

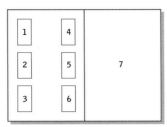

1, 2 and 3. Freestanding and wall mirrors from the series "BLACK" designed by Sara Mano for PnP■

4. Mirror with container cupboard and lamp from Gedy■

The cupboard is in stainless steel and the lamp in chrome-plated brass and glass■

5. Cupboard with door from the collection "ALUMINIUM". Design from Jonathan Daifuku for Cosmic■

Made in anodized aluminum in matt silver■

6. Accessories "FLINT". Design from Massimo Morozzi for PnP■

Made in plastic and available in four different colors■

7. Toilet and bidet "WELCOME" and bathtub "LAVASCA MINI". Designs from Matteo Thun. Table lamp "MOMY" and its miniature wall version "BABY" from Georges Adatte. All from Rapsel■

The sanitaryware is manufactured in black or white ceramic. The WC top can be equipped with a perfume dispenser and music■

Following pages:
Bathroom completely furnished with articles designed by Philippe Starck. The sanitaryware and accessories are manufactured by Duravit and the faucets and shower column by Axor (Hansgrohe). The oval bathtub is in sanitary acrylic■

FAUCETS
the control of water

Water is life. And it is a resource that is becoming scarcer and scarcer. Statistics indicate that only 2% of all of the water on the planet is drinkable. What is more, it has been suggested that it could become the petroleum of the 21st century. That is to say, that each and every one of the inhabitants of the earth (particularly those that live in industrialized countries) should start to become more aware of the quantity of water they consume a day and begin to value each drop as if it were a precious gift from nature.

Bearing this in mind, we have a greater appreciation of what has been achieved by the advances in faucet technology. A faucet that drips, or which uses a greater caudal than necessary or that has to be on for five minutes before hot water comes out is almost an attack on the environment. As a result, the choice of faucets becomes an important decision when it comes to decorating the bathroom because a faucet is no longer merely a water outlet.

Among the most recent technical innovations brought forward by this area, the systems that allow for the caudal and temperature to be regulated which leads to optimizing the consumption of water and energy stand out. This means that in addition to respecting the environment an important saving in economic terms is also achieved. Many of the latest thermostats obtain the desired temperature in a question of a few seconds in addition to incorporating various security systems to avoid possible scolding. Whatever the case, and to be sure that the faucet chosen complies with the expectations of use and consumption, its manufacture should comply with the European quality certification ISO 9001.

Then, what is it that makes a good faucet? Ecology, in as much as an optimum use of natural resources; the quality of its components, which makes the initial investment worthwhile, and which is measured in terms of resistance, permanence, and durability; the ergonomics that augment the degree of comfort in its use; and, evidently, aesthetics in as much as the creation of harmonious forms that are in keeping with the surroundings and able to persist in time. Technology and design unify to bring about a new generation of faucets that in addition to improving their functionality, become a medium which allows users to differentiate themselves and express their personality. Since the Danish architect and designer Arne Jacobsen and the company Vola set off on the path of innovation in this sector in 1969 with the presentation of the mythical faucet KV1, an authentic renovation of the language used up until then in the bathroom, this instrument – which grants the control of water to man – has never ceased to be improved and perfected.

Jacobsen's designs persist on the market as icons of mastery from twentieth-century design. They are found along with creations from the avant-garde such as electronic faucets activated by means of infrared rays or models with incorporated lights not to mention the new systems of showers that allow the user to choose from a variety of water flows. All of this intensifies her revitalizing historical role.

An awareness of water as a purifying and ritual element seems to have a greater presence than ever in the bathrooms of today and it has become the outstanding feature of this space. The incorporation of faucets that enhance well being and that wager for the conservation of water, the source of life, is, from this point of view, an effective declaration of love of this most valuable element.

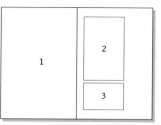

Imagen página 139:
Showerhead from the "RAINDANCE" series. Design from Phoenix Product Design form Hansgrohe.

1. Single-lever mixer with shower-head from the series designed by Arne Jacobsen for the company Vola. Manufactured in chrome-plated brass. The elements that make up the series can be combined in many different ways.

2. Single-lever washbasin faucet "PUMPY". Design from Peia for Cisal.

3. Bathtub thermostat "TERMOLUX" from Ramón Soler.
Allows water volume and temperature to be regulated manually. Includes an anti-scolding device and pressure balance valve that automatically corrects variations in temperature in less than two seconds.

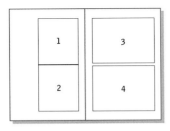

1 and 2. Single-lever and classical mixer faucets for washbasins from the collection "Axor Citterio" designed by Antonio Citterio for Axor (Hansgrohe)▪
All of the models from this collection are available finished in chrome or platinum galvanoplastic (as used in jewelry)▪
3. Single-lever shower mixer with diverter and hand-held showerhead from the series designed by Arne Jacobsen for Vola▪
4. Two-handled wall faucet for washbasin from the series designed by Arne Jacobsen for Vola▪

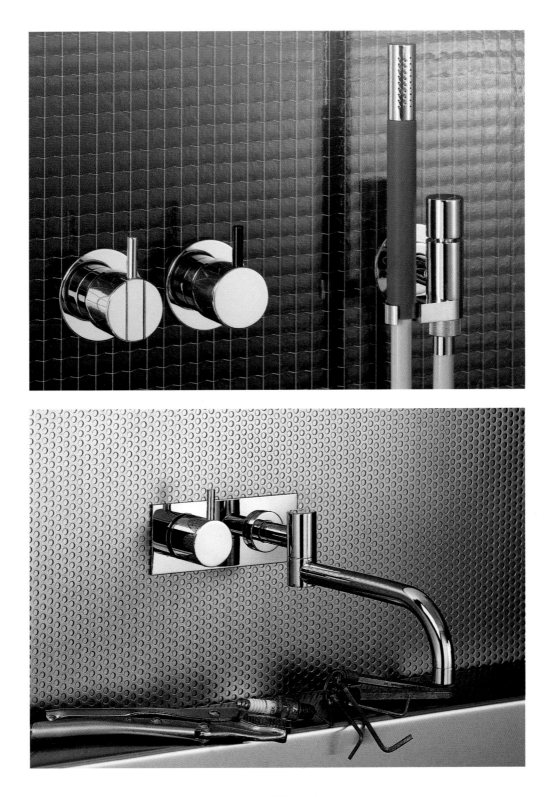

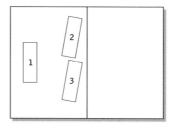

1. Shower faucet "RAINDANCE ALL-ROUNDER". Design from Phoenix Product Design for Hansgrohe▪
The handshower is combined with a vertical support that converts it into a fixed shower as well as into a lateral shower jet. The head offers five different sorts of water jet including a rain simulator▪
2. Rail shower set "UNICA RAINDANCE". Design from Phoenix Product Design for Hansgrohe▪
The rail fitted to the wall and its extensive support allow overhead or lateral showers to be enjoyed that can be easily adapted to user's height▪
3. Fixed and handshower "TERRANO" from the collection Axor Showerpipes from Axor (Hansgrohe)▪
Combination of fixed shower with large head along with hand-held head with thermostat and diverter inspired in classical designs▪
4. Single-lever faucet for bathtub from the program "IL BAGNO ALESSI". Design from Stefano Giovannoni for Alessi and produced by Oras▪

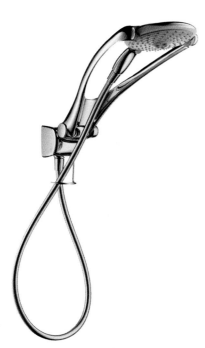

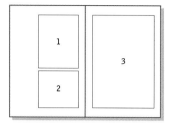

1. Thermostatic shower mixer "EDEN" combined with the shower set "ERMES" from Cisal■

2. Mixer and handshower from the collection "PAOLO E FRANCESCA". Design from Alberto Rizzi and Rossano Didaglio for Ritmonio■

3. Composition "COMBI 1" made up of twin-handled mixer with six lateral water jets, single-lever mixer with handshower and magnetic soap dish from the series designed by Arne Jacobsen for Vola■

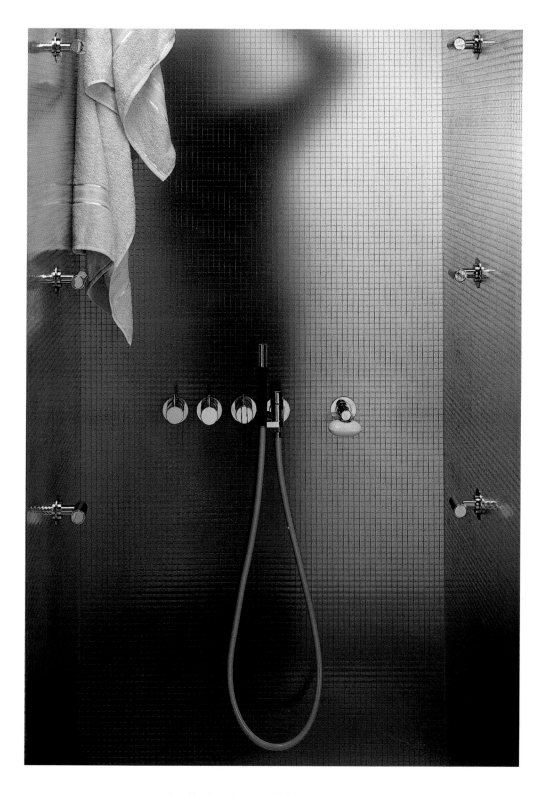

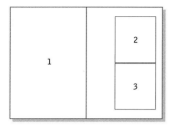

1. Transparent single-lever wash-basin faucet with incorporated light "Brick". Distributed by Trentino
2. Single-lever washbasin mixer "Kobe" from Buades
Incorporating extendable lever, flexible alimentation tubes, automatic ventilation and drainage
3. Single-lever washbasin faucet "Kermess" de Gessi

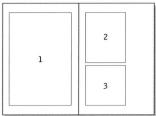

1. Single-lever mixer "HV1" with small lever and fixed spout with water-saving aerator from the series designed by Arne Jacobsen for Vola∎
2. Single-lever wall mixer with long spout "IsyContract". Design from Matteo Thun with Antonio Rodríguez for Zucchetti∎
This innovative collection is characterized by its tendency to occult the essential and for creating a modular system that allows for a maximum flexibility in composition. Among other prizes and mentions, it has received the "Red Dot Award-Product Design 2002"∎
3. Single-lever mixer "Font" from Gessi∎

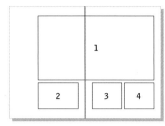

1. Bathroom environment which integrates various models of washbasins, bathtubs and showers from the faucet collection "Axor Citterio" designed by the architect Antonio Citterio for Axor (Hansgrohe)▪
2. Mixer for bath and handshower in flexible metal,1.7 m long, from the series "Loft" from Roca▪
3. Two-handled washbasin faucet from the collection Antonio Miró Bathroom created by the mentioned designer and produced by Supergrif▪ This collection of faucets consists of 32 different models to take into account all of the possible needs a bathroom may have▪
4. Single-lever bidet faucet from the program "Il Bagno Alessi". Design from Stefano Giovannoni for Alessi and produced by Oras▪

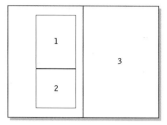

1. Single-lever washbasin faucet from the collection "DIAMETROTREN-TACINQUE" designed by Davide Berce-lli for Ritmonio▪

This series offers more than 40 solutions for the washbasin▪

2. Single-lever faucet for bath, with rotating spout, and handshower attachment from the program "IL BAGNO ALESSI". Design from Stefano Giovannoni for Alessi and produced by Oras▪

3. Single-lever shower faucet from the collection "D38". Design from Roviras and Torrente for Supergrif▪

This collection has been awarded the Design Plus ISH Prize 2003 by the IF Industrie-Forum Design, Hannover▪

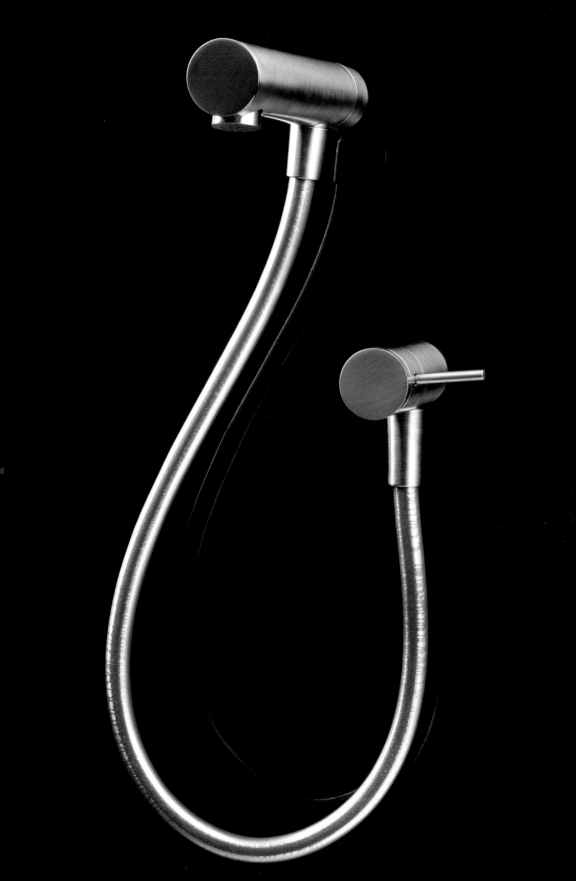

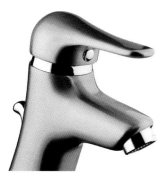

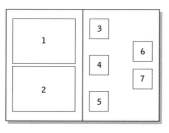

1. Single–lever washbasin faucet "Di-
verso" from Gessi■

2. Single–lever washbasin faucet
"Romance" from Gessy■

3. Single–lever faucet "Delfos"
from Supergrif■

4. Two-handled washbasin mixer
with automatic draining from the series "Loft" from Roca■

5. Single–lever washbasin mixer with
prolongation from the series "Spin"
from Raúl Barbieri for Zucchetti■

6. Two-handled washbasin faucet set
from the series "Tangent". Design
from E. Carulla and B. Stearns for
Supergrif■

7. Single–lever washbasin faucet from
the series "Odisea" from Ramón So-
ler■

Finished in matt chrome■

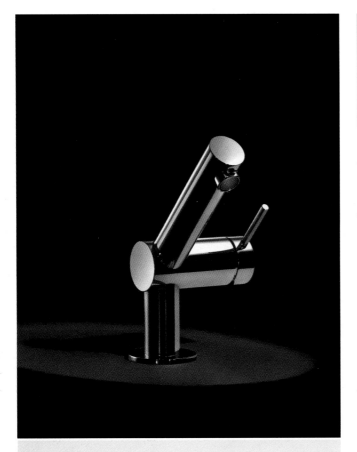

1		3
2		

1. Single—lever washbasin faucet with flexible spout "CONTROL" from Xavier Claramunt and Miguel de Mas for Cosmic■
Incorporates systems to control water flow and temperature in a rational way■
2. Two-handled washbasin mixer from the collection Antonio Miró Bathroom created by the mentioned designer and produced by Supergrif■ The faucet collection is made up of 32 different models that combine finishes in chrome with natural materials such as wood and rubber■
3. Washbasin faucets with levers from the collection "AXOR CITTERIO" designed by Antonio Citterio for Axor (Hansgrohe)■
The metal plate located below the faucets is a distinctive feature of this line. All of the models from this collection are available finished in chrome or in platinum galvanoplastic■

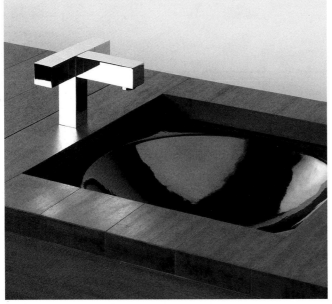

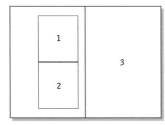

1 and 2. Single-lever mixer for wash-basin and thermostat and mixer for bath and shower from the series "FRAME". Design form Massimiliano della Monaca and Davide Vercelli for Ritmonio▪

Stainless steel structure and flexible tube covered in transparent PVC. Design Plus Prize▪

3. Shower set "MINIMAL" from Cisal▪

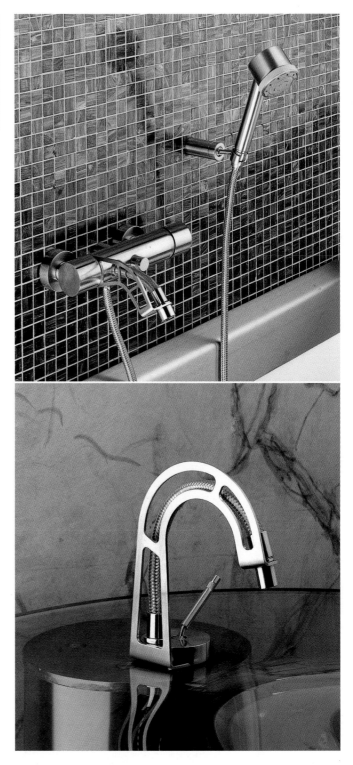

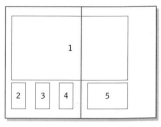

1. Single-lever translucent washbasin faucet with incorporated light "BRICK". Distributed by Trentino■ Available with different light tones, in white or completely transparent■
2 and 4. Single–lever faucets "SILVER SPIRIT" and "SILVER CROWN" from the Silver Series from Roca■ The model "SILVER SPIRIT" is presented finished in chrome with a transparent lever■
3. Single–lever washbasin faucet "OMEGA". Design form Inés Jackson for Supergrif■
5. Washbasin faucets from the collection Antonio Miró Bathroom. Idea by Antonio Miró and produced by Supergrif■ This collection of faucets consists of 32 different models to take into account all of the possible needs a bathroom may have■

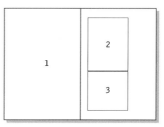

1. Washbasin faucets from the series "MEM" developed by Sieger Design in collaboration with the Meiré y Meiré agency for Dornbracht.
These faucets are characterized by their wide flat spouts that do away with the usual aeration achieving a water flow that imitates the sensation of water that bubbles out of a spring.
2. Washbasin faucets from the series "ATRIO" from Grohe.
Incorporates exclusive ceramic disks, Carbodur®, which are as hard as diamonds and that guarantee optimum smoothness for many years.
3. Washbasin taps from the collection "TARA CLASSIC" designed by Sieger Design for Dornbracht.

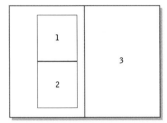

1. Single-lever washbasin faucets from the collection "DIAMETROTREN-TACINQUE" designed by Davide Bercelli for Ritmonio■
This series offers more than 40 solutions for washbasins■
2. Single-lever washbasin faucets from the collection "DREAMSCAPE". Design from Michael Graves for Dornbracht■
3. Single-lever washbasin faucets "OXIGEN" from Gessy■

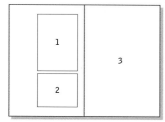

1. Showers with flexible heads "SIR BISS". Design from Marcello Ziliani for Wonderful World■

2. Thermostat "GROHTHERM 3000" from Grohe■

Allows for the simultaneous control of three functions: the water volume, flow and output as much for the bath as for the handshower. Incorporates a "security button" at 38° Celsius to prevent possible scolding and an "ecological button" that diminishes the water volume in as much as 50%■

3. Shower system from the collection "AXOR CITTERIO". Design from the architect Antonio Citterio for Axor (Hansgrohe)■

Combines a fixed shower with handshower so that different sensations can be enjoyed in a minimum of space■

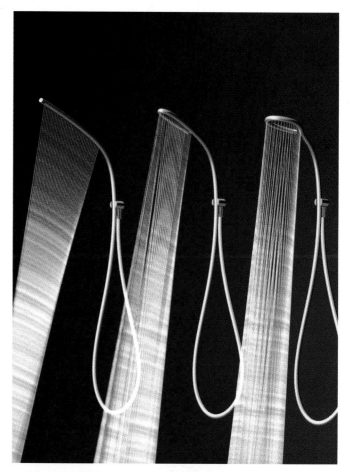

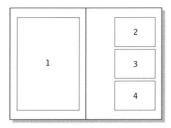

1. Single-lever mixer with fixed spout from the series designed by Arne Jacobsen for Vola■

2. Single-lever built-in mixer from the collection "ODISEA" from Ramón Soler■

3. Single-lever mixer "QUADRO" from Gessy■

4. Single-lever mixer with fixed spout from the collection "DIAMETROTRENTACINQUE". Design from Davide Vercelli for Ritmonio■

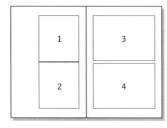

1. Single-lever washbasin faucet from the collection "BELLE DE JOUR" developed by Sieger Design for Dornbracht.
2. Standard washbasin faucets from the collection "DREAMWORKS" designed by the architect Michael Graves for Dornbracht.
3. Bathroom atmosphere in which the faucets for washbasin and bathtub from the collection "Axor Citterio" designed by the architect Antonio Citterio for Axor (Hansgrohe) stand out.
4. Built-in washbasin faucet set from the series "ISYARC". Design from Matteo Thun with Antonio Rodríguez for Zucchetti.
This model includes cross-shaped handles along with a curved spout inspired in more classical forms.

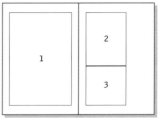

1. Wall washbasin faucet set with infrared controls from the series "EMOTE". Design from Sieger Design for Dornbracht■
2. Single-lever washbasin faucet with high spout "OZONE" from Gessi■
3. Single-lever washbasin faucet "PROFUMI" from Gessi■

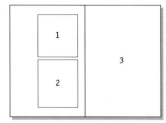

1. Single-lever washbasin faucet from the series "QUADRO" from Gessi▪
2. Washbasin mixer from the collection "META PLASMA". Design from Sieger Design for Dornbracht▪
This new line stands out for its eye-catching colors. The body of the mixer element is manufactured in chrome-plated brass covered in matt colored acrylic▪
3. Single-lever washbasin faucet "FANTAGHIRO" from Gessi▪

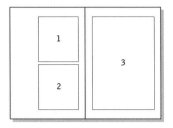

1. Single-lever bath mixer with integrated handshower from the series with built-in cylinder "IsyStick". Design from Matteo Thun and Antonio Rodríguez for Zucchetti■
2. Shower system "Freehander" from the line "Grohetec" from Grohe■ This system allows for the water jets to be redirected as desired so that different types of shower and massages can be obtained. Awarded the Design Plus Prize by the IF Industrie-Forum Design, Hannover■
3. Bath faucet set from the collection "Axor Citterio" designed by Antonio Citterio for Axor (Hansgrohe)■
The metal plate, finished in chrome or in platinum galvanoplastic, located under the faucet set with cross-shaped handles is one of the distinctive features of this series■

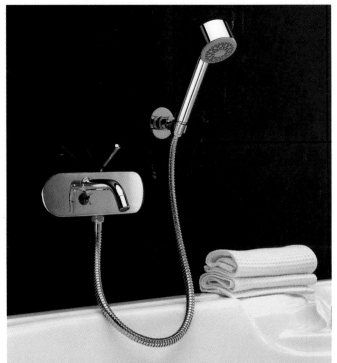

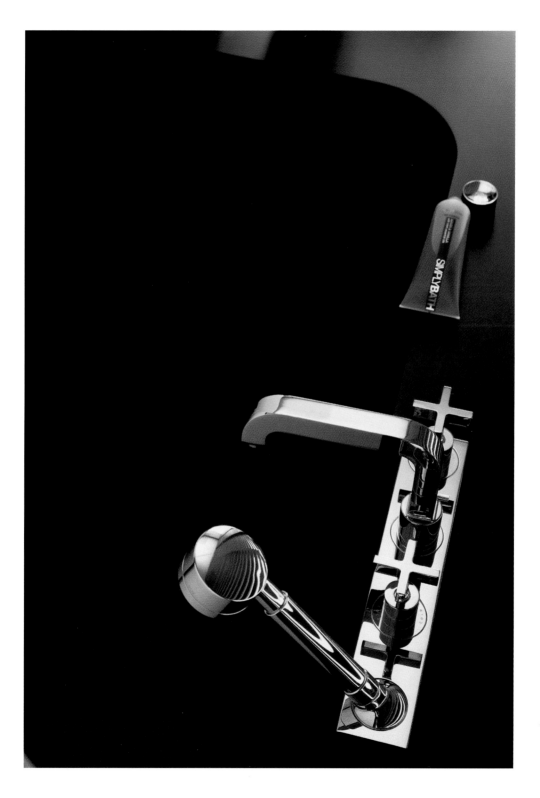

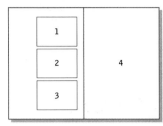

1. Single-lever mixer for bath and shower "ELAN" with diverter integrated in the design. From Buades.
2. Single-lever mixer with bathtub spout with handshower and shower support from the series designed by Arne Jacobsen for Vola.
3. Thermostatic mixer "STYLO" for bath and shower from Buades. Relocates position of bath shower diverter to the mouth of spout creating a highly-stylized design. Incorporates "ECO" system with a control mechanism that rotates 270° to permit smoother water flow selection.
4. Large-headed fixed shower from the "RAINDANCE" line from Phoenix Product Design for Hansgrohe. The water jet simulates the effects of rain and gives a soft relaxing massage.

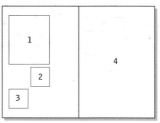

1. Built-in thermostat for bath and shower "SELECT" from Buades■
Both water flow and output are governed by just one control thanks to the two ceramic disks. The new build-in anti-water-filtration system permits the use of non-anti-humidity materials such as those frequently used in partition walls■

2. Washbasin faucet with incorporated liquid soap dispenser "WATER-POT" designed by Marcello Ziliani with Gabrielle Pezzini. Produced by Krover■

3. Single-lever bath and shower faucet "SUPERMIX" from Ramón Soler■

4. A stylized design for this washbasin faucet from the collection "D38" FROM Roviras and Torrente for Supergrif■
This collection was awarded with the Design Plus ISH 2003 Prize by the IF Industrie-Forum Design, Hannover■

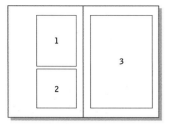

1. Two-handled faucet from the collection "DIAMETROTRENTACINQUE" designed by Davide Bercelli for Ritmonio▪

This series consists of more than 40 solutions for the bathroom▪

2. Single-lever washbasin faucet "STEP" from Cisal▪

3. Original single-lever washbasin faucet finished in matt chrome from the collection "PAOLO E FRANCESCA". Design from Alberto Rizzi and Rossano Didaglio for Ritmonio▪

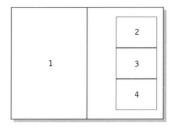

1. Washbasin faucet set model "BARCELONA". Design from Peia for Cisal▪

2. Washbasin facets from the series "MEM" developed by Sieger Design in collaboration with the agency Meiré y Meiré for Dornbracht▪
These faucets are characterized by their wide flat spouts that do away with the usual aeration achieving a water flow that imitates the sensation of water that bubbles out of a spring▪

3. Single-lever washbasin mixer from the series "FRAME". Design from Massimiliano della Monaca and Davide Vercelli for Ritmonio▪
Stainless steel structure and interior flexible tube covered with transparent PVC. Design Plus ISH Prize, 2003 awarded by the IF Industrie-Forum Design, Hannover▪

4. Single-lever washbasin faucet "MAGIC" from Cisal▪

FLOORS
AND WALLS
playing with colors and textures

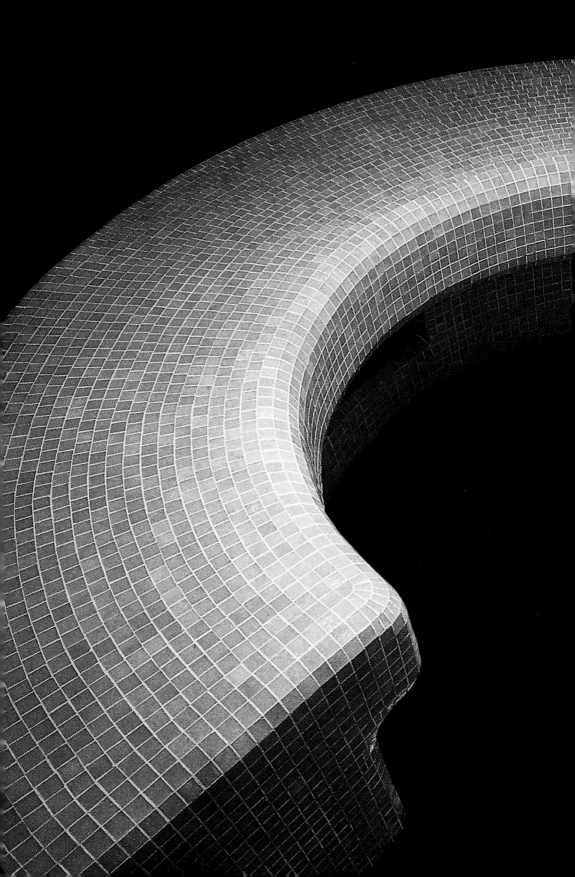

The materials that cover the walls and floor in this "humid room" are much more than simply facings or surfaces in the same way that a dress is much more than something to cover a woman's body. Floor tiles and wall tiles align to give a personality to the bathroom. They are like a second skin that gives this space a life of its own, a space that breathes, transforms, transmits sensations.

Our sense of smell and our sense of touch are stimulated by these surfaces: the softness of glazed ceramic tiles, the roughness of natural stone just wanting to be touched, the authenticity of earth converted into clay blocks, the transparency of mosaic, the intensity of the colors in ceramic, the expressiveness in the painting, the artistic content in hand-illustrated ceramic, the pleasure of walking barefoot over wood or over a marble floor, enjoying direct contact with nature, ... Textures and colors which possess an ability to relax or stimulate the mind according to the combinations chosen.

Earth, fire and water unit with glass and color to offer an infinite number of shades hues and tints that are presented in a comparable number of sizes. As a result, the possibilities for combinations are practically infinite and can be adjusted to any type of decorative style, taste, personality or way of life. Although the objective always tends to be the same: to create an environment of wellbeing that favors the flourishing of positive emotions.

Over the last few years, there has been a revival of artisanal techniques and traditional building materials, which, although it may seem to be paradoxical, are produced using the latest technologies. As a result, these innovative techniques are applied to the creation of pieces that take us back to the past. This is especially true in the case of porcelain tiles that imitate natural materials and that of vitrified mosaic which has the same degree of expressive force it had hundreds of years ago. In many cases, the value of each piece lies in it being unique thanks to the vein or particular tonalities that make it impossible to find another that is alike.

This return to an artisanal presence is symptomatic of current trends that encourage society to rediscover its origins and introduce spaces that are able to recreate nature within the home without a loss to contemporaneity. In this way, according to new bathroom culture, these walls and floors with a rustic reminiscence are perfectly able to live side by side with the purest minimalism or tastes that are more classical by nature.

In addition to aesthetic considerations (plain colors or printed designs, warm or cold, mat o brilliant, with borders and decorative trimmings or with no concession to ornamentation, with an aged feel or avant-garde feel, soft or rough textures, highly polished or simply brushes surfaces, slate or metal, ...), there are others of a more practical nature that should also be taken into account.

The floors and walls have to offer a high level of durability and resistance to wear and tear. In general, the quality in here is measured in terms of resistance to humidity, abrasive products, brusque changes of temperature, knocks and frequent use, percentages of water absorption or invulnerability to staining, scratching and breaking. It is also advisable to include an anti-slip treatment to the floors.

As always, function before beauty and durability before the ethereal to create, in this place of intimacy, a second skin able to perpetuate in time and maintain its practicability intact along with its capacity to stimulate our senses.

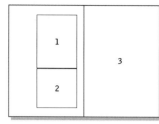

Photograph page 191:
Glass mosaic from the series "VET-
RICOLOR" from Bisazza▪

1. Glass mosaic "VETRICOLOR 20"
from Bisazza▪
Made up of square beveled-edged
pieces 2 × 2 cm and 4 mm thick
glued over paper or mesh▪
2. Mosaic from the collection
"CHIARA" from Jasba▪
This model has the unusual measurements of 5 × 2.4 cm. The mosaic is protected with "HYDROTECT" to
maintain its shine and keep it germ
free▪
3. Composition with mosaic from the
model "M2" from Jasba▪
The pieces of mosaic measure 2.4 ×
2.4 cm. The mosaic is protected with
"HYDROTECT" to maintain its shine
and keep it germ free▪

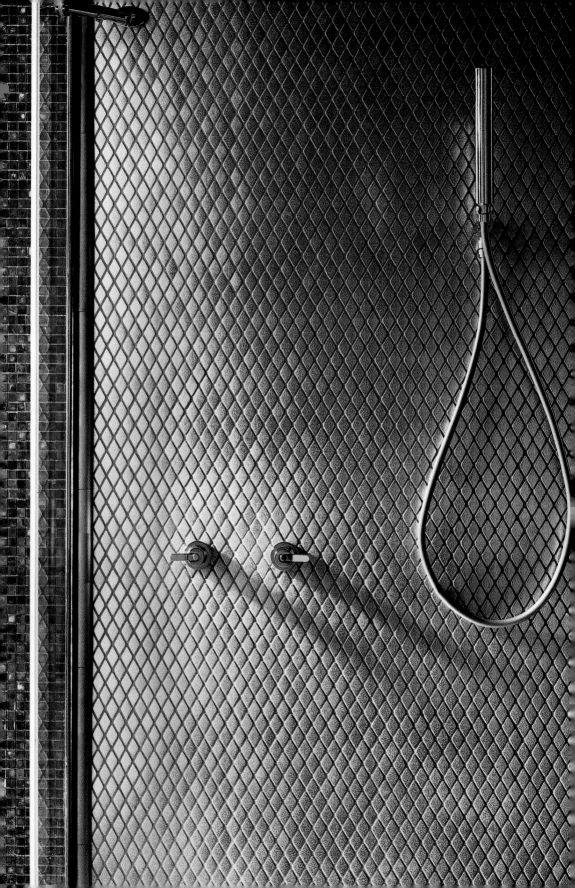

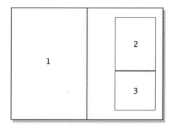

1. Exclusive mosaic with metallic finish from the collection "META-LLISMO" from Sicis■
Manufactured in stainless steel and brass over a rubber support. It does not rust; it is resistant to staining and scratching, lightweight and extremely flexible. Available in a multitude of formats and sizes■
2. Mosaic "JEANS" developed by United Colors of Benetton in collaboration with the Marazzi group■
The range of colors in this collection has been inspired in the different tones offered by denim jeans■
3. Mosaic and tiles from the collection "SOLITAIRE" from Jasba■
The pieces of mosaic measure 5 × 5 cm and the tiles 31.2 × 41.8 cm■

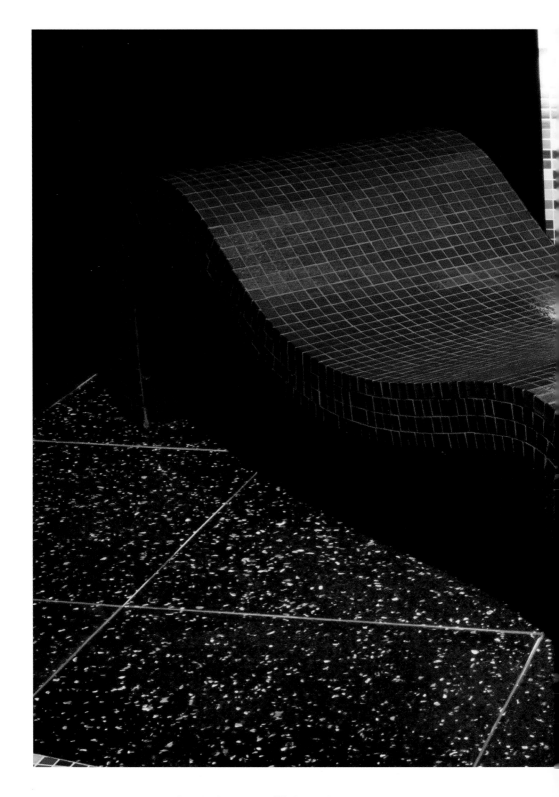

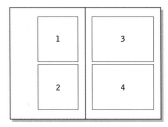

Previous pages:
Combination of different models of mosaic in intense colors and flooring with an agglomerate made up of crushed fragments of recycled quartz and granite. From the firm Trend■

1. Bathroom in travertine marble Albero with decorative boarder "CORINTO". From L'Antic Colonial (Porcelanosa)■
2. Wall in aged clay mosaic, 2 × 2 cm pieces, and flooring in aged clay with decorative square-grid in white marble. From L'Antic Colonial (Porcelanosa)■
3. Combination of various flooring and walling collections from the firm Keraben■
4. Tiles and ceramic mosaic from the series "GALAXY" with a soft combination of colors. De L'Antic Colonial (Porcelanosa)■

1. Collection of hand-made ceramic "Roses" designed by Carolyn Quatermaine and produced by Gabbianelli. The tiles are decorated by means of transfers. Available over a white background or over a hand-painted base. Measurements: 20 × 20 cm.

2. Decorative tiles with designs from Piero Fornasetti "Soli e lune", for the shower area, and "Architetture" for the washbasin wall. Produced by Cerámica Bardelli.

3. Tiles "Gay Pride", with the slightly wrinkled gloss finish "Riflessi & Riflessi", designed by the Studio Davide Pizzigoni and produced by Cerámica Bardelli.

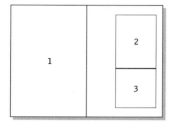

1. Wall and flooring from the series "LESS DARK" from Trentino.
2. Flooring with incrustations of glass pearls. Distributed by Trentino.
3. Glass tiles, available in many colors and sizes, from Trentino.

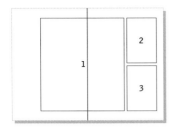

1. Ceramic wall and flooring white body tiles from the collection "LE PRECIOSE" that imitate marble. From Cerim Ceramiche (Florim Ceramiche)■

2. Walling in travertine marble slabs, 30 × 60 cm, with small border in stainless steel and washbasin "FORO". From L'Antic Colonial (Porcelanosa)■

3. Combination of tiles and travertine marble mosaic and mosaic trimmings in green. From L'Antic Colonial (Porcelanosa)■

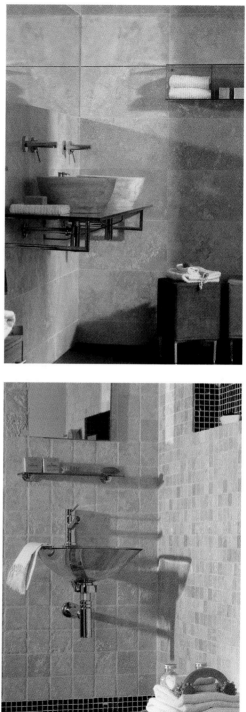

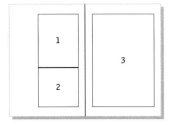

1. Walling from the model "Perú" from the collection Colore&Colore with smooth high-gloss finish. Design from the Studio Davide Pizzigoni for Cerámica Bardelli▪
2. Tiles from the collection "La Terra", 20 × 20 cm format, hand painted and available in 12 colors. From Gabbianelli▪
3. Tiles in various sizes from the model "Pompeiano", with the slightly wrinkled gloss finish "Riflessi & Riflessi", designed by the Studio Davide Pizzigoni and produced by Cerámica Bardelli▪

<table>
<tr><td rowspan="2">1</td><td>2</td></tr>
<tr><td>3</td></tr>
</table>

1. Mosaic with metallic finish from the collection "METALLISMO". Exclusive from Sicis■

Manufactured in stainless steel and brass over a rubber support. It does not rust; it is resistant to staining and scratching, lightweight and extremely flexible. Available in a multitude of formats and sizes. In this photograph, it has been combined with vitreous mosaic from the collection Sicis■

2. Combination of tiles from the series "Solitaire" with mosaics that measure 2.4 × 2.4 cm. From Jasba■

3. Glass mosaic from the collection "LE GEMME" from Bisazza■

Avventurina, a synthetic stone developed in Venice during the 17th century, is used in its elaboration■

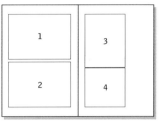

1. Fine porcelain flooring from the collection "DEDICATO A GAUDÍ" inspired in the work of this outstanding architect. From Rex Ceramiche Artistiche■

2. Flooring in a classical style from Trentino■

3. Wall and flooring designed by Claudio La Viola for Brix■

4. Tiles decorated with motifs from the series "TEMA E VARIAZIONE 1" designed by Piero Fornasetti. Produced by Cerámica Bardelli■

There are 20 different designs. The decoration is in platinum over a white background, in a format of 10 × 10 cm and with matt or gloss finishes■

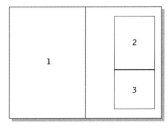

1. Bathroom completely done out in the glass mosaic "VETRICOLOR" with a sprinkling of white gold mosaic in 2 × 2 cm pieces. The mirror frames are in white gold mosaic in 1 × 1 cm pieces. From Bisazza■
The glass and gold mosaic in formed by a sheet of 24k gold set between two pieces of glass for its protection. This atmosphere is a project from the architects Carlo dal Vianco and Mauro Braggion■
2. Walling and flooring from the collection "ARDESIE" that is made up of slates with diverse geological characteristics and different finishes. From Ceramiche Marazzi■
3. Glass mosaic "VETRICOLOR 20" with a format of 2 × 2 cm. From Bisazza■

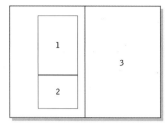

1. Glass mosaic in diverse sizes and finishes from the collection from Trend.

2 and 3. Two compositions created with a combination of glass mosaics from the collection "VETRICOLOR" and "LE GEMME". From Bisazza.

The mosaics from the series "LE GEMME" are elaborated by craftsmen with Avventurina, a synthetic stone developed in Venice during the 17th century.

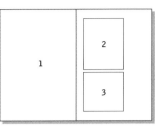

1	2	
	3	

1. Glass tiles from Trentino.
2. Walling in porcelain stoneware tiles from the collection "AREA" from Floor Gres (Florim Ceramiche).
3. Porcelain stoneware tiles that imitate natural stone textures from the collection "CRATER ROCK" from Cerim Ceramiche (Florim Ceramiche).

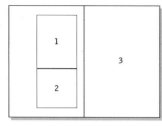

1. Walling in black and white marble mosaic in pieces that measure 3 × 5 cm and are 1 cm thick. From L'Antic Colonial (Porcelanosa)∎
2. Walling from the series "MARMI BLANCO", produced by Porcelanosa, and flooring "BADEN ÁMBAR" produced by Venis∎
3. Walling with borders in vitreous mosaic with a pearly finish alternated with mosaic with metallic finish from the collection "METALLISMO". Produced by Sicis∎

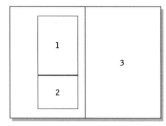

1. Walling and flooring in different models from the collection of mosaic with metallic finishes "METALLIS-MO" from Sicis■
In this composition, the mosaics finished in stainless steel are alternated with others finished in polished brass■
2. Glass tiles from Trentino■
3. Tiles "PROVENZA", with the Slightly wrinkled gloss finish "RIFLESSI & RIFLESSI", designed by the Studio Davide Pizzigoni and produced by Cerámica Bardelli■

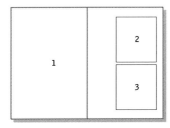

1. Bathroom done out in tiles from the collection "Petra Aeterna" from Iris Cerámica■
Made in porcelain stoneware imitating textures from natural stone■
2. Walling and flooring in porcelain stoneware from the series "Touch Stone" that imitates textures and aspects of natural stone. From Rex Ceramiche Artistiche (Florim Ceramiche)■
3. Tiles from the "Wave" collection from Brix■

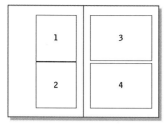

1. Wall and flooring from the series "OXON" from Porcelanosa∎
2. Tiles "MINIMAL NAVY", with the rough gloss finish "RIFLESSI & RIFLESSI", designed by the Studio Davide Pizzigoni and produced by Cerámica Bardelli∎
3. Wall and flooring in white body tiles that imitate marble from the collection "DIVINA" from Cerim Ceramiche (Florim Ceramiche)∎
4. Walling from the collection "HAPPENING" in ceramic from the series Semigres®. From Iris Cerámica∎

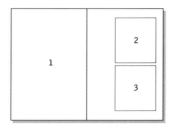

1. Mirror frame covered in tiles from the collection "SOLITAIRE", in a format of 5 × 5 cm, with different decorative designs. From Jasba■

2. Collection of double-fired tiles "IL FUOCO", in format 20 × 20 cm. From Gabbianelli■

Hand-painted and available in 12 colors■

3. White body wall tiles produced in one firing and that imitate natural stone from the collection "WESTERN STONE" from Cerim Ceramiche (Florim Ceramiche)■

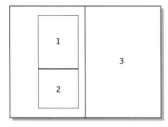

1. Ceramic covering from the collection "LA BELLE MAISON" from L'Antic Colonial (Porcelanosa)∎
2. Walling in stoneware ceramic from the collection "I PARCHI MARINI" from Ceramiche Ragno (Grupo Marazzi)∎
3. Wall and flooring in stoneware ceramic from the collection "LE MAGIE". Available in five colors. From Ceramiche Ragno (Grupo Marazzi)∎

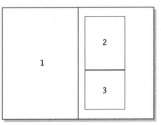

| 1 | 2 |
| | 3 |

1. Shower walls in glass mosaic from the collection "LE GEMME" manufactured with Avventurina, a synthetic stone developed in Venice during the 17th century. From Bisazza.
2. Tiles and mosaics from the collection "SOLITAIRE" from Jasba.
3. Tiles from the model "LOFT" from Cerámica Bardelli.

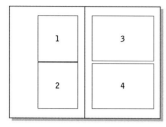

| 1 | 3 |
| 2 | 4 |

1. Flooring in porcelain stoneware and walling in the ceramic product Semigres® from the collection "TO BE CASUAL" from Iris Cerámica.
2. Wall and flooring tiles in various sizes from the collection "PASO" from Jasba.
3. Wall and flooring from the "HAPPENING" collection in ceramic from the series Semigres®. From Iris Cerámica.
4. Tiles with incrustations of platinum or white colored mosaic from the collection "SOLITAIRE" from Jasba.

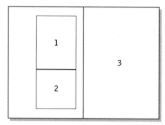

1. Tiles and matching border from Porcelanosa∎

2. White body wall and floor tiles from the collection "LE PREZIOSE" that imitate marble. From Cerim Ceramiche (Florim Ceramiche)∎

3. Wall and flooring from the collection "MARMO" in fine porcelain with an aged finish that gives it the appearance and texture of marble. From Rex Ceramiche Artistiche (Florim Ceramiche)∎

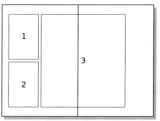

1. Wall and flooring with the texture of natural stone from Keraben▪

2. Mosaic with metallic finish from the collection "METALLISMO" from Sicis▪

Manufactured in stainless steel and brass over a rubber support. It does not rust; it is resistant to staining and scratching, lightweight and extremely flexible. Available in a multitude of formats and sizes▪

3. Composition with different elements from the collection "TIZIAN" from Jasba▪

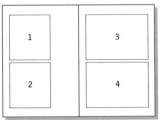

1. Wall and flooring from the collection "SLATE" in porcelain stoneware glazed in a rustic style. From Keraben▪

2. Slate flooring "NEPAL" and walling in natural stone "TIBET" from L'Antic Colonial▪

3. Flooring in porcelain stoneware and walling in the ceramic product Semigres® from the collection "TO BE ELEGANT" from Iris Cerámica

4. Wall and flooring from the collection "COLONIALE" in fine porcelain stoneware inspired in cream-colored marbles. From Floor Gres (Florim Ceramiche)▪

Following pages:
Wall and flooring from the collection "MARMO" in fine porcelain with an aged finish that gives it the appearance and texture of marble. From Rex Ceramiche Artistiche (Florim Ceramiche)▪

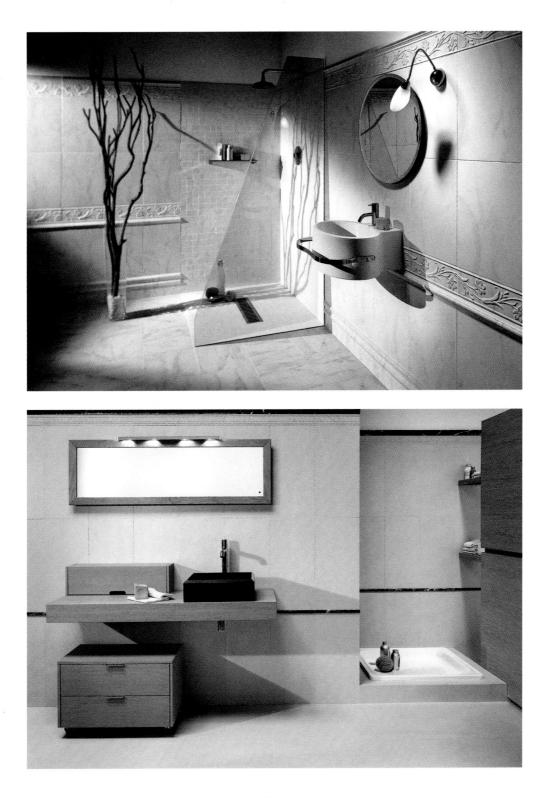

HYDROMASSAGE BATHS
AND SHOWERS
wellness – the new culture of wellbeing

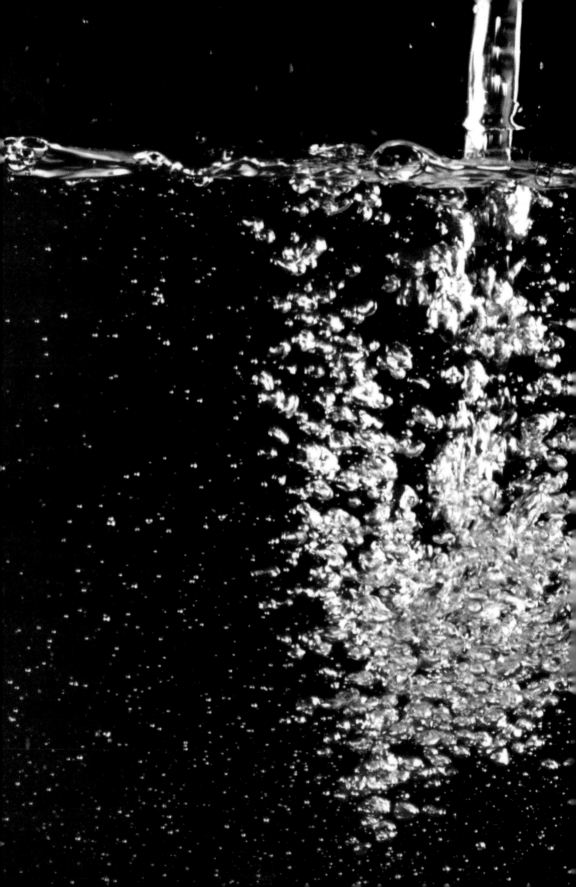

The union of water and heat as a source of regeneration is a practice that goes back many centuries. The Greco-Roman culture with its popular collectively-used hot baths (some of which are still in existence), was what stimulated the practice of public steam baths as a means of regenerating the body and mind. As a result, this Mediterranean tradition of cleansing and purification are found in the origins of these present hydromassage systems and in all apparatus encompassed in the term "wellness" that has been developed to achieve an authentic state of wellbeing.

The concept is not new. It is the technology that is new.

Since the first hydromassage bathtub was created for therapeutic use by Roy Jacuzzi 40 years ago, the application of ever increasing technological innovations along with increasingly defined designs have led to a situation in which all the strength of the old culture of wellbeing elevated to its maximum potential can be recreated in the intimacy of our own bathrooms. Hydromassage bathtubs and shower cabins have become a kind of leisure center in the very heart of our homes, true private temples to relaxation which include all sorts of features.

From a massage proportioned by jets of air and water to the psychological effects of chromotherapy or aromatherapy, there is a great range of things that can be demanded from a bathroom along with their corresponding benefit over the organism. Some functions that can be included in our "wellness machines" are a steam bath, Finnish sauna, musictherapy, an ultrasound system of hydromassage (patented by Teuco), a gymnasium, electronic temperature control or, simply, a shower nozzle that allows you to control the kind of water jet along with the caudal. The properties of the principal wellbeing systems are as follows:

—Hydromassage: applied by means of jets integrated in the structure of the bathtub or in the column of the shower. There are innumerable models on the market that can adapt to all sorts of tastes and budgets. The majority incorporate disinfecting and cleaning systems that increase the security of the bath and lengthen the life of the apparatus. The energetic massage provided by jets of air, water, or a combination of both tones up muscles, relaxes the epidermis, stimulates the metabolism and the circulation of both blood and lymph, improves treatments for rheumatic and orthopedic pains and it is, without a doubt, an effective antidote for stress and states of fatigue in general not to mention the energy and freshness that it brings.

–Steam sauna: this is a feature offered by some shower cabins. Taken on a regular basis this can alleviate pains that are rheumatic in nature, improve respiratory problems, stimulate blood circulation, relax muscular tension, combat cellulitis, tone up and tighten skin so as to delay the appearance of wrinkles and reestablish a psychophysical equilibrium.

–Chromotherapy: the properties of light and color have a direct influence on how we feel. They effect metabolism and psychic well being. Administering determined colors over our body for a few minutes has a repairing and stimulating effect. It has been scientifically proven that red stimulates, orange revitalizes, yellow is a sedative and green a relaxant.

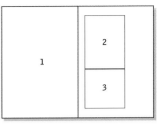

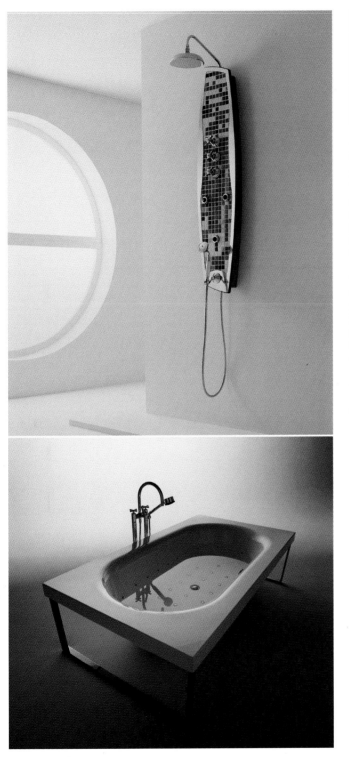

1. Overhead shower from the series "BALANCE MODULES" developed by Sieger Design for Dornbracht.
The shower becomes regenerating rain or an energetic cascade with this new system of modules that imitate sensations experienced in nature.

2. Column shower "CIBELES" designed by Francis Montesinos for Hidrobox.
The wall tiles combine with the wooden base and stainless steel. Measurements: 145 cm high × 31 cm wide.

3. Hydromassage bathtub "KAOS", belonging to the Floyd line, designed by Roberto and Ludovica Palomba for Kos.
Freestanding acrylic bathtub designed to be situated in the center of the bathroom. It is supported exclusively by two legs and does away with side panels.

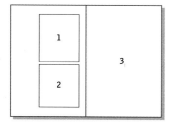

1. Shower panel "HELIS". Design from Phoenix Product Design for Phâro (Hansgrohe)■
Version for corner installation with translucent glass base. Incorporates fixed shower, handshower, five adjustable lateral jets and halogen spotlight■
2. Multifunctional shower cubicle "DOCCIAVISION" from Teuco■
Made in transparent blue metacrylate. In addition to the massage jets, it incorporates a steam sauna and thermostatic mixer. The glass is treated with Clean Glass to help with cleaning and maintenance■
3. Multifunctional shower cubicle "KOSMIC", from the Floyd series, designed by Roberto and Loduvica Palomba for Kos■
Incorporates a steam sauna and Idrocolore®, a system for chromotherapy■

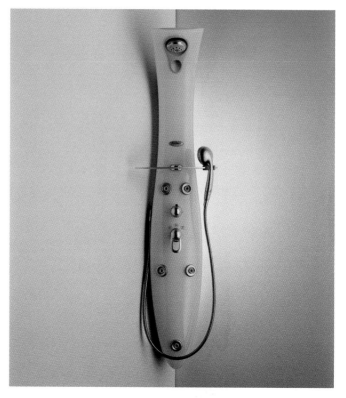

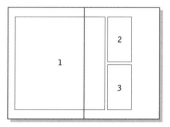

1. Shower system formed by the acrylic shower tray "FLOOR" with a polished metal structure and tempered glass panel. Part of the Floyd series designed by Roberto and Ludovica Palomba for Kos▪

2. Hydromassage bathtub with headrest suitable for two persons. A design from Philippe Starck for Duravit▪

3. Shower column "NIAGARA" from Baños 10▪

Measurements: 196 cm high × 49.5 cm wide▪

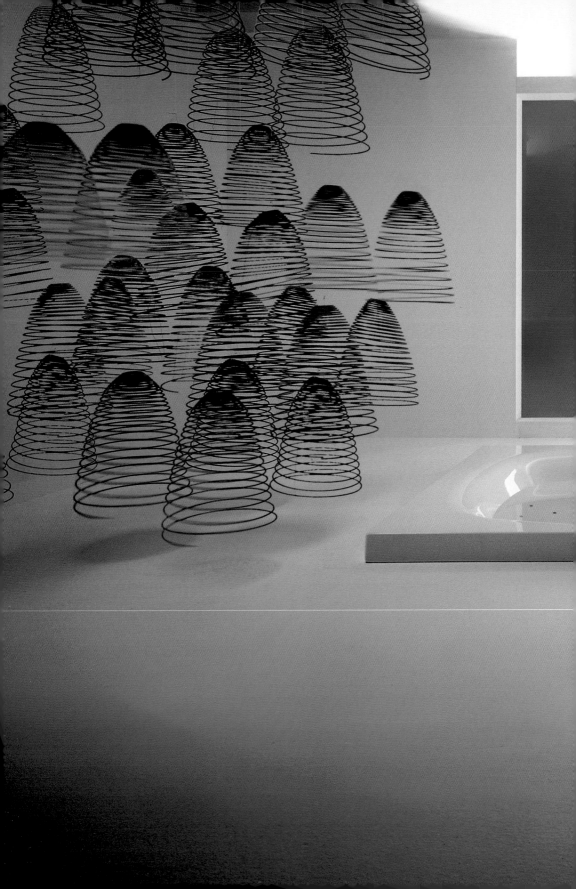

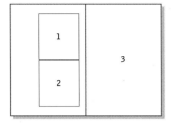

Previous pages:
Built-in hydromassage "Kaos", from the Floyd series, designed by Roberto and Ludovica Palomba for Kos■

1. Hydromassage bathtub "Iman" from Baños 10■
Functions are controlled from an incorporated digital panel and the bath can also be equipped with different systems. Measurements: 190 cm long × 155 cm wide■

2. Hydromassage bathtub "Judith" from Baños 10■
The inside of the bathtub has been designed in ergonomic forms to guarantee the user's comfort. Equipped with a digital control panel for functions■

3. Multifunction shower cubicle with sauna and chromotherapy system "Evolution" form Teuco■
The walls and oval formed door are made in hydrorepellent tempered glass. The shower tray is in Duralast® (composite of silica quartz and acrylic resin). The cubicle is large enough for two people■

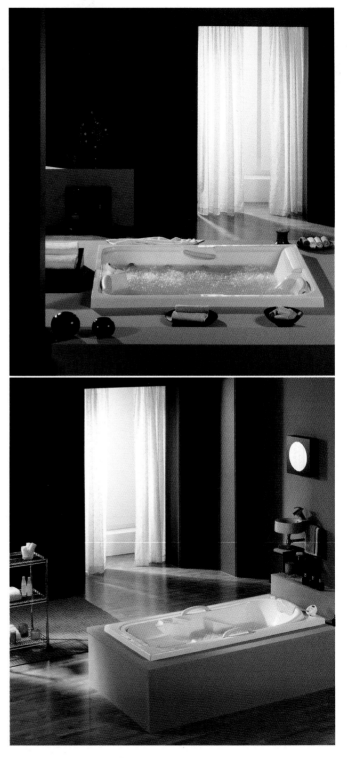

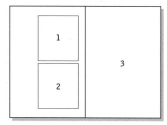

1. Hydromassage bathtub "MIRAN-DA" from Hidrobox▪
Incorporates six directional water jets, 14 nozzles, security system and the possibility to integrate other additional optional systems. Measurements: 190 cm in length × 110 cm in width▪
2. Round hydromassage bathtub "CASARCA" developed by Remo Jacuzzi for Hidrobox▪
Incorporates six jets, 18 nozzles, security system and the possibility to integrate various additional optional systems. Measurements: 183 cm in diameter▪
3. Round hydromassage bathtub with wooden support "OSAKA" from System-Pool▪

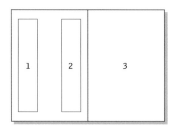

1. Shower panel "HELIS". Design from Phoenix Product Design for Phâro (Hansgrohe)∎
Version in translucent white. Incorporates fixed shower, handshower, five directional side jets, thermostat with faucet and diverter and halogen spotlight∎
2. Multifunction shower column from Teuco∎
Made in DuralLight or tempered semitransparent glass. Available in various colors and finishes and in wall or angle version∎
3. Shower column "GALLERY" from Cisal∎

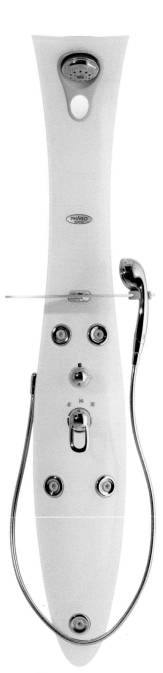

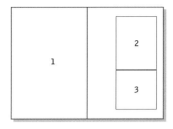

1. Angular Finnish sauna "CARIBE" from Hidrobox▪
Unipersonal sauna with heat generator. Measurements: 219 cm in height × 90 cm in width × 90 cm in length▪

2. Hydromassage bathtub "NEW ANGELICA" designed by Remo Jacuzzi for Hidrobox▪
Incorporates six jets, two air regulators and 18 nozzles. A diversity of optional systems can be integrated such as the aromatherapy accessory or self-cleaning system. Measurements: 182 cm in length × 122 cm in width▪

3. Hydromassage bathtub "TARIM 177" from Revita (Grupo Sanitec)▪
Incorporates digital function control panel, headrest, six water and air jets and 14 air nozzles. Ideal for small spaces. Measurements: 170 cm in length × 70 cm in width▪

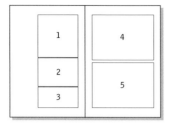

Previous pages:
Hydromassage column "Aquakit
Iris" from Roca∎
Base in translucent glass combined
with aluminum. Incorporates halogen lamp, five multifunctional directional jets, thermostatic control, two
shelves, fixed shower with five functions and handshower∎

1. Hydromassage bathtub "Atenea"
designed by Remo Jacuzzi for
Hidrobox∎
Incorporates six jets, six rotating
mini-jets for the neck, two air regulators, 16 nozzles and various optional accessories such as an aromatherapy system. Measurements: 183 cm
in length × 107 cm in width∎
2. Acrylic hydromassage bathtub
from the series "Quattro" from Bellavista.
Incorporates six water/air jets and
ten air jets, electronic control panel,
light and water heating. Measurements: 180 cm in length × 100 cm in
width∎
3. Hydromassage bathtub "Vivo-
Vario" from Kaldewei∎
Incorporates a combined air and water system with 22 nozzles in the
bottom or sides. In the bottom nozzles, water is mixed with hot air which
creates millions of tiny bubbles.
Equipped with a self-disinfecting
system∎
4. Hydromassage bathtub with light
from the series "Starck" designed
by Philippe Starck for Duravit∎
5. Hydromassage bathtub "Kaos",
from the Floyd line, designed by
Roberto and Ludovica Palomba for
Koss∎
Freestanding acrylic bathtub with
steel base equipped with the chromotherapy Idrocolore® system∎

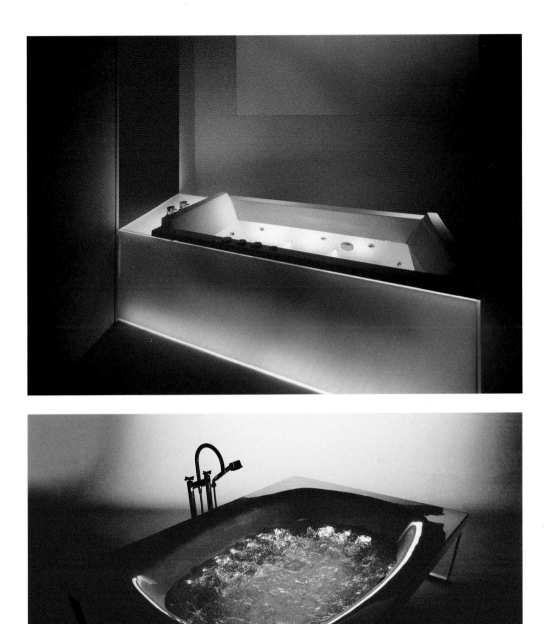

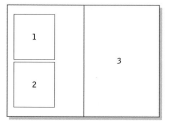

1. Shower "DeLuxe". Design from Phoenix Product Design for Phâro (Hansgrohe)■
Integrates steam generator, aroma dispenser, fixed shower, handshower, six side jets, chromotherapy system, loudspeakers and cascade shower■
2. Shower and steam sauna cubicle with sliding doors "Aquafun De-luxe" from Phâro (Hansgrohe)■
Incorporates electronic controls, steam generator, seat, aromatherapy, chromotherapy and music. Available in three tray sizes: 75, 85 or 95 cm■
3. Shower and steam sauna cubicle from the bathroom collection designed by Norman Foster. Produced by Hoesch■
Integrates steam generator, two seats and side jets. Measurements: 225 cm in height × 160 cm in width■

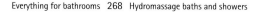

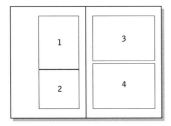

1. Shower cubicle "PLUVIA 100 R" designed by Claudio Papa for Albatros (Grupo Sanitec)∎
Integrates digital control panel, steam generator, aromatherapy, light, music, foot massage and 18 sequential vertical and back jets∎
2. Hydromassage bathtub "MYLIFE" from the series created by the firm Frog. Produced by Teuco∎
This bath stands out as a result of its innovative design that combines acrylic with wood. Available in freestanding version, to be built in or attached to the wall. It can be equipped with the high-frequency hydromassage system Hydrosonic, an exclusive from Teuco∎
3. Hydromassage bathtub "ZENIT" from System-Pool∎
Original design for a freestanding bathtub that combines acrylic with a wooden platform∎
4. Bathtub "KUSATSU" designed by Sottsass Associati for Kaldewei∎
This design has been directly influenced by Japanese bath culture. It has an unusually deep seat (81 cm) that allows the user to completely submerge in the water. Manufactured in enameled steel. Available with the optional hydromassage system "TRIPLUS". Awarded with the Design Plus Prizes∎

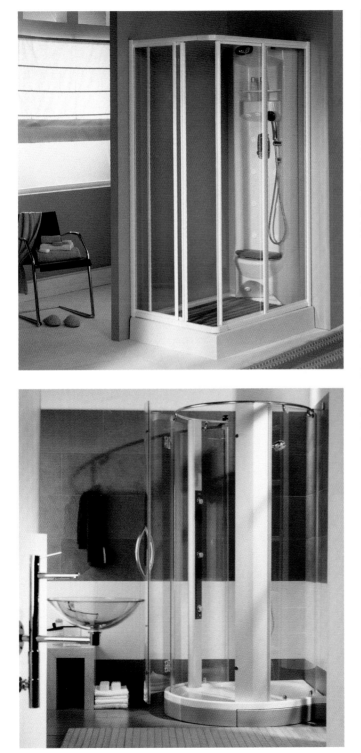

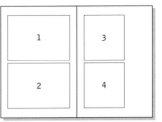

1. Shower "115" with steam sauna from Phâro (Hansgrohe)■
Equipped with fixed shower, hand-shower, four side water jets, steam generator, illumination, enameled steel tray and glazed sides■
2. Built-in hydromassage bathtub "Rondò" from Teuco■
Designed to incorporate the exclusive Hydrosonic system. This consists of eight hydrosonic jets that emit ultra-sound massaging waves by means of a special patented nozzle that combines the flow of water and air with the emission of an ultrasonic wave-band. Measurements: 181 cm in length × 111 cm in width■
3. Shower cubicle "Box" from Baños 10■
Incorporates steam generator and is available in various finishes and sizes■
4. Completely transparent shower cubicle "Prisma" from System-Pool■

1	3
2	4

1. Hydromassage bathtub "ZERO". Design from Adolf Babel for Hoesch. Incorporates a novel reclining backrest with integrated jets that provide a deep massage in the areas of the back and feet while protecting the vertebral column▪

2. Hydrosauna "AURUM" from Roca▪ Cubicle with two differentiated zones equipped with glass dividers, central column in anodized aluminum and acrylic shower tray▪

3. Angular hydromassage bathtub, with underwater light, "OUVERTURE" from Teuco▪ Frontal with colored-glass window. Incorporates the Hydrosonic ultrasound hydromassage system that acts on a cellular level▪

4. Acrylic bathtub with hydromassage from the series "ARQ. COLLECTION" from Gala▪

DAVID HOCKNEY: A
THE METROPOLITAN M

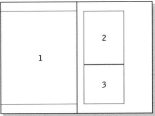

1. Hydromassage bathtub "ARUBA" with optional shower column. From Roca∎
Fabricated in Polimetil (sanitary metacrylate). Measurements: 170 × 170 cm∎

2. Hydroshower equipped with Hydrosonic system "SINTESI" from Teuco∎
Units the benefits of the ultrasound hydromassage system with those of the multifunctional shower. The cubicle incorporates a glass sliding door∎

3. Fitness equipment with integrated shower and sauna cubicle from the program "FITNESS CORNER" from Teuco∎
Allows for a wide range of fitness exercises to be carried out while controlling the main training parameters by means of an electronic control panel. Complemented with the benefits of sauna and shower. Available with a large number of accessories∎

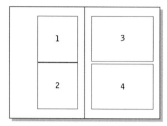

1. Shower column "AGOYAN" from the series Aluminium from Baños 10■
Measurements: 140 cm in length × 25 cm in width■
2. Shower column "RUACANA" with wooden base. From Baños 10■
Measurements: 154 cm in height × 34 cm in width■
3. Hydromassage "AQUAKIT HOTEL'S" from Roca■
Made in anodized aluminum. Includes handshower with four functions, two jets for neck, two back jets, one lumbar jet and option for full bath. The jets provide two types of massage: constant or of regulable intensity■
4. Shower "STEAM" designed by Phoenix Product Design for Phâro (Hansgrohe)■
Equipped with steam generator, overhead shower, handshower, six side jets, cascade shower, foldable seats and loudspeakers■

Following pages:
Shower column "ISLA" from Phâro (Hansgrohe)■
Finished in matt anodized aluminum. Includes two side jets, thermostat, diverter and handshower. Measurements: 2.15 m in height■

DIRECTORY

ALAPE
Am Gräbicht 1-9
D-38644 Goslar
GERMANY
Tel. 49 (0) 5321 558-0
Fax. 49 (0) 5321 558 -199
www.alape.com

ALBATROS-DOMINO SPA
(SANITEC GROUP)
Via Valcellina, 2 - Z. Ind. Nord
33097 Spilimbergo (PN)
ITALY
Tel. 39 0427 587111
Fax. 39 0427 50304
www.albatros-idromassaggi.com

ALESSI
Via Privata Alessi, 6
28882 Crusinallo (VB)
ITALY
www.alessi.com

ALESSI
(distributed in Spain by Manuel
Echevarria, S.L.)
Gran Via de Carlos III, 158
08034 Barcelona
SPAIN
Tel. 34 932 051 420
E-mail: mechevarria@futurnet.es

ALTAMAREA BY TECNOLAC SRL
Via Istria 1/3 z.i.
31046 Oderzo (Treviso)
ITALY
Tel. 39 0422 713212
Fax. 39 0422 816818
www.altamareabath.it

ALTHEA CERAMICA
Zona Ind. Loc. Prataroni
01033 Civita Castellana (VT)

ITALY
Tel. 39 0761 542144
Fax. 39 0761 542129
www.altheaceramica.com

ALTRO
La Coma 18 A1 P.L.
Pla de Santa Ana
080272 Sant Fruitós de Bages
(Barcelona)
SPAIN
Tel. 34 938 789 890
Fax. 34 938 789 043
www.altro.es

ART CERAM
Via Monsignor Tenderini snc
01033 Civita Castellana (VT)
ITALY
Tel. 39 0761 599499
Fax. 39 0761 514232
www.artceram.it

ARTQUITECT
C/ Dolors Graners, 79
08440 Cardedeu
(Barcelona)
SPAIN
Tel. 34 938 444 070
Fax. 34 938 444 071
www.artquitect.net

ARTQUITECT (Show-room):
C/ Comerç, 31
08003 Barcelona
SPAIN
Tel. 34 932 683 096
Fax. 34 932 687 773
E-mail: shor-room@artquitect.net

AXIA
Via delle Querce, 9
31033 Castelfranco Veneto

(Treviso)
ITALY
Tel. 39 0423 496222
Fax. 39 0423 743733
www.axiabath.it

AXOLO
Viale Lombardia 83
22063 Cantú (CO)
ITALY
Tel. 39 031 734270
Fax. 39 031 734271
www.axolo.it

BAÑOS 10
Ctra. Viver -Pto. Burriana,
Km. 58.4
P.O. Box 27
12200 Onda
(Castellón)
SPAIN
Tel. 34 964 626 940
Fax. 34 964 626 009
www.banos10.com

BELLAVISTA
CERÁMICAS DE BELLAVISTA S.A.
Avda. Andalucía, 228
41700 Dos Hermanas
(Sevilla)
SPAIN
Tel. 34 955 675 157
Fax. 34 955 675 979
www.bellavista.com

BERTOCCI
Via Petrosa, 24
50019 Sesto Florentino
(Florencia)
ITALY
Tel. 39 055 44929
Fax. 39 055 446770
www.bertocci.it

BISAZZA SPA
Viale Milano, 56
36041 Alte (Vicenza)
ITALY
Tel. 39 0444 707511
Fax. 39 0444 492088
www.bisazza.it

BISAZZA ESPAÑA
Showroom: C/ Fusina, 11
08003 Barcelona
SPAIN
Tel. 34 936 014 012
Fax. 34 936 014 013

BOFFI
Via Oberdan, 70
20030 Lentate sul Seveso
ITALY
Tel. 39 0362 5341
Fax. 39 0362 565077
www.boffi.com

BUADES (GRUPO TEKA)
Conquistador 2
07350 Binissalem
(Mallorca)
SPAIN
Tel. 34 971 870 210
Fax. 34 971 870 211
www.buades.com

CERAMICA BARDELLI
Via Pascoli, 4/6
20010 Vittuone (MI)
ITALY
Tel. 39 02 9025181
Fax. 39 02 90260766
www.bardelli.it

CERAMICA CATALANO
S.P. Falerina Km. 7,200
01034 Fabrica di Roma (VT)
ITALY
Tel. 39 0761 5661
Fax. 39 0761 574304
www.catalano.it

CERAMICA GLOBO
Località La Chiusa

01030 Castel Sant Elia
(VT)
ITALY
Tel. 39 0761 516568
Fax. 39 0761 515168
www.ceramicaglobo.com

CERAMICHE MARAZZI
Viale Regina Pacis, 39
41049 Sassuolo (MO)
ITALY
Tel. 39 0536 860111
Fax. 39 0536 860644
www.marazzi.it

CERAMICHE RAGNO
Viale Virgilio 30
41100 Modena
ITALY
Tel. 39 059 384111
Fax. 39 059 384444
www.ragno.it

CERASA SRL
Via Borgo Nobili 19
31010 Bibano di Godega di
Sant Urbano
(TV)
ITALY
Tel. 39 0438 783411
Fax. 39 0438 783450
www.cerasa.it

CERIM CERAMICHE
(FLORIM CERAMICHE SPA)
Via Canaletto, 24
41042 Fiorano (MO)
ITALY
Tel. 39 0536 840911
Fax. 39 0536 840999
www.cerim.it

CISAL RUBINETTERIA
Via P. Durio, 160
28010 Pella Frazione Alzo
(Novara)
ITALY
Tel. 39 0322 918111
Fax. 39 0322 969518
www.cisal.it

COLOMBO DESIGN
Via Baccanello, 22
24030 Terno d'Isola
(BG)
ITALY
Tel. 39 035 4949001
Fax. 39 035 905444
www.colombodesign.it

INDUSTRIAS COSMIC, S.A.
C/ Cerdanya, 2 - Pol. Ind.
La Borda; Apdo. Correos 184
08140 Caldes de Montbui
(Barcelona)
SPAIN
www.icosmic.com

DORNBRACHT
Köbbingser Mühle, 6
D-58640 Iserlohn
GERMANY
Tel. 49 0 2371 433 0
Fax. 49 0 2371 433 232
www.dornbracht.com

DORNBRACHT ESPAÑA S.L.
C/ Bruc 94, 2° 2ª
08009 Barcelona
SPAIN
Tel. 34 932 723 910
Fax. 34 932 723 913
www.dornbracht.com

DURAT
(TONESTER LTD)
Huhdantie 4
FIN-21140 Rymättylä
FINLAND
Tel. 358 2 252 1000
Fax. 358 2 252 1022
www.durat.com

DURAVIT AG
Postfach 240
D-78128 Hornberg
GERMANY
Tel. 49 7833 70-0
Fax. 49 7833 8585
www.duravit.com
info@duravit.de

DURAVIT ESPAÑA, S.L.
C/ Balmes, 184, 4° 1ª
08006 Barcelona
SPAIN
Tel. 34 932 386 020
Fax. 34 932 386 023
www.duravit.com

FLAMINIA
s.s.Flaminia, Km. 54,630
01033 Civita Castellana (VT)
ITALY
Tel. 39 0761 542030
Fax. 39 0761 540069
www.ceramicaflaminia.it

FLOOR GRES
(FLORIM CERAMICHE SPA)
Via Canaletto, 24
41042 Fiorano (MO)
ITALY
Tel. 39 0536 840 111
Fax. 39 0536 844750
www.floorgres.it

GABBIANELLI
S.S. 143 Loc. Vergnasco
13882 Cerrione (Bi)
ITALY
Tel. 39 015 6721
Fax. 39 015 671626
www.gabbianelli.com

GALA CERAMICAS
Ctra. Madrid-Irún, km. 244
Apdo. 293 - 09080 Burgos
SPAIN
Tel. 34 947 474 100
Fax. 34 947 474 103
www.gala.es

GAMADECOR
(GRUPO PORCELANOSA)
Ctra. Viver-Pto. Burriana, Km. 62
12540 Villarreal
(Castellón)
SPAIN
Tel. 34 964 506 596
Fax. 34 964 506 596
www.gama-decor.com

GEDY SPA
Via Dell'Industria 6
Zona Industriale
21040 Origgio (VA)
ITALY
Tel. 39 0296 9501
Fax. 39 0296 950201
www.gedy.com

GEDY IBERICA S.A.
Bernat Metge, 110
08205 Sabadell
(Barcelona)
SPAIN
Tel. 34 937 122 377
Fax. 34 937 119 308
www.gedyiberica.es

GESSI
Via Marconi 27/A
13037 Serravalle Sesia (VC)
ITALY
Tel. 39 0163 451711
Fax. 39 0163 459273
www.gessi.it

GESSI
(DISTRIBUTED IN SPAIN BY
ORPAN S.A.)
Av. Del maresme, 209, bajos 2°
08301 Mataró
(Barcelona)
SPAIN
Tel. 34 937 906 686
Fax. 34 937 906 844
E-mail: orpan@ie-orpan.es

GROHE ESPAÑA S.A.
C/ Botánica, 78-88-Pol. Pedrosa
08908 L'Hospitalet de Llobregat
(Barcelona)
SPAIN
Tel. 34 933 368 850
Fax. 34 933 368 851
www.grohe.es

HANSGROHE
Riera Can Pahissa 26B
08750 Molins de Rei (Barcelona)
SPAIN

Tel. 34 936 803 933
Fax. 34 936 803 909
www.hansgrohe.es

HATRIA
Viale Virgilio 30
41100 Modena
ITALY
Tel. 39 059 384567
Fax. 39 059 384212
www.hatria.com

HIDROBOX
Pol. Ind. Belcaire, P-709
P.O. Box 73
12600 Vall de Uxo
(Castellón)
SPAIN
Tel. 34 964 691 825
Fax. 34 964 691 922
www.hidrobox.es

HOESCH DESIGN
(HÜBNER KONCEPT, S.L.)
Rbla Josep Tarradellas, 1, Local 4
08860 Castelldefels
(Barcelona)
SPAIN
Tel. 34 936 342 191
Fax. 34 936 342 239
www.hoesch.de

HOESCH GMBH & CO.
Postfach 10 04 24
D-52304 Düren
GERMANY
Tel. 49 2422 54-0
Fax. 49 2422 6793
www.hoesch.de

INDA
Via XXV Aprile 53
21032 Caravate (VA)
ITALY
Tel. 39 0332 608111
Fax. 39 0332 619317
www.inda.net

IRIS CERAMICA
Via Ghiarola Nuova 119

41042 Fiorano Modese
ITALY
Tel. 39 0536 862111
Fax. 39 0536 804602
www.irisceramica.it

JASBA-DEUTSCHE
STEINZEUG
KERAMIK GмвH
Im Petersborn 2
D-56244 Ötzingen
GERMANY
Tel. 49 (0) 2602 682-0
Fax. 49 (0) 2602 682 -1625
www.deutsche-steinzeug.de

KALDEWEI GMBH & CO
Beckumer Straße 33-35
D-59229 Ahlen
GERMANY
Tel. 49 (0) 2382 7850
Fax. 49 (0) 2382 785200
www.kaldewei.com

KERABEN
Ctra. Valencia-Barcelona
Km. 44.3
12520 Nules
(Castellón)
SPAIN
Tel. 34 964 659 500
Fax. 34 964 674 245
www.keraben.com

KERAMAG
(SANITEC GROUP)
Kreuzerkamp, 11
D-40878 Ratingen
GERMANY
Tel. 49 (0) 2102 /9 16-0
Fax. 49 (0) 2102/ 9 16-245
www.keramag.com

KOS
Viale de la Comina 17
33170 Pordenone
ITALY
Tel. 39 0434 363405
Fax. 39 0434 551292
www.kositalia.com

KOS -(KURAT TRADE-
DELEGATION IBERIAN
PENINSULA)
Llança 39, 10° 2ª
08015 Barcelona
SPAIN
Tel. 34 93 2266914
Fax. 34 93 226 50 63
E-mail: kurattrade@terra.es

KOZIOL
Werner-von-Siemens-Str. 90
D-64711 Erbach / Odenwald
GERMANY
Tel. 49 (0) 6062 604-273
Fax. 49 (0) 6062 604-258
www.koziol.de

L'ANTIC COLONIAL
(GRUPO PORCELANOSA)
Camino «Les Voltes» s/n
12540 Villarreal
(Castellón)
SPAIN
Tel. 34 964 534 545
Fax. 34 964 523 861
E-mail:
anticcolonial@anticcolonial.com

LAUFEN
Wahlenstrasse 46
CH-4242 Laufen
SWITZERLAND
Tel. 41 61 765 7111
Fax. 41 61 765 5111
www.laufen.ch

MARCELLO ZILIANI
Via Amba d'Oro, 68
25123 Brescia
ITALY
Tel. 39 030 363 758
Fax. 39 030 360 430
www.marcelloziliani.com

MILLDUE
Via Balegante, 7
31039 Riese Pio X (Treviso)
ITALY
Tel. 39 0423 755233

Fax. 39 0423 456319
www.milldue.it

NITO ARREDAMENTI
Via E. Mattei, 19
53041 Asciano (Siena)
ITALY
Tel. 39 0577 718899
Fax. 39 0577 718733
E-mail: nitoarredamenti@tin.it

OML
Via G.B. Fattori, 57
42044 Gualtieri (Reggio Emilia)
ITALY
Tel. 39 0522 828798
Fax. 39 0522 828355
www.oml.it

ORAS
Isometsäntie 2; P.O. Box 40
FIN-26101 Rauma
FINLAND
Tel. 358 0 2 8361
Fax. 358 0 2 831 6300
E-mail: www.oras.com

OUTLOOK ZELCO
Via Rocca, 9
24030 Presezzo (Bergamo)
ITALY
Tel. 39 035 603511
Fax. 39 035 464823
www.outlookzelco.com

PERMESSO (DISTRIBUTOR
INTERNATIONAL ORPAN S.A.)
Av. Del maresme, 209, bajos 2°
08301 Mataró
(Barcelona)
SPAIN
Tel. 34 937 906 686
Fax. 34 937 906 844
E-mail: orpan@ie-orpan.es

PNP SRL
Via Artigiani, 6
25014 Castenedolo (BS)
ITALY
Tel. 39 030 2739807

Fax. 39 030 2130201
www.pnpshop.it

POM D'OR
(BLANCH CRISTAL, S.A.)
Pol. Ind. Camí Ral; C/ Galileo, 11
08850 Gavá
(Barcelona)
SPAIN
Tel. 34 935 565 120
Fax. 34 935 565 122
www.blanchcristal.com

PORCELANOSA
Ctra. Nacional 340, km. 55,8
Apdo. Correos 130
12540 Villarreal
(Castellón)
SPAIN
Tel. 34 964 507 140
Fax. 34 964 507 141
www.porcelanosa.com

POZZI-GINORI SPA
(SANITEC GROUP)
Via Valcellina, 2 - Z. Ind. Nord
33097 Spilimbergo (PN)
ITALY
Tel. 39 0427 587111
Fax. 39 0427 50304
www.pozzi-ginori.com

Q'IN
Via E. Curiel, 20
50063 Figline Valdarno
(Firenze)
ITALY
Tel. 39 055 9154138
Fax. 39 055 9154139
www.qin.it

RAMÓN SOLER
Vallespir 26;
Pol. Ind. Fontsanta
08970 Sant Joan Despí
(Barcelona)
SPAIN
Tel. 34 933 738 001
Fax. 34b 933 737 858
www.ramonsoler.net

RAPSEL
Via Volta, 13
20019 Settimo Milanese (Mi)
ITALY
Tel. 39 02 3355981
Fax. 39 02 33501306
www.rapsel.it

REGIA
Via Vigevano, Zona Industriale
20053 Taccona di Muggiò (Mi)
ITALY
Tel. 39 278 2510
Fax. 39 278 2571
www.regia.it

REVITA-DOMINO SPA
(SANITEC GROUP)
Via Valcellina, 2-Z. Ind. Nord
33097 Spilimbergo (PN)
ITALY
Tel. 39 0427 587111
Fax. 39 0427 50304
www.revita-idromassaggi.com

REX CERAMICHE ARTISTICHE
(FLORIM CERAMICHE SPA)
Via Canaletto, 24
41042 Fiorano (MO)
ITALY
Tel. 39 0536 840811
Fax. 39 0536 840816
www.rex.cerart.it

RITMONIO RUBINETTERIE SRL
Via Indren, 4-
Zona Ind. Roccapietra
13019 Varallo (VC)
ITALY
Tel. 39 0163 560000
Fax. 39 0163 560100
www.ritmonio.it

ROCA
Avda. Diagonal, 513
08029 Barcelona
SPAIN
Tel. 34 933 661 200
Fax. 34 934 194 501
www.roca.es

SAMUEL HEATH
Leopold Street
B12 0UJ Birmingham
UNITED KINGDOM
Tel. 44 121 772 2303
Fax. 44 121 772 3334
www.samuel-heath.com

SANICO
PORCELANAS S.L.
Navarra 14
46008 Valencia
SPAIN
Tel. 34 963 826 664
Fax. 963 826 298
www.sanico.es

SICIS
Via M. Monti 9/11
48100 Ravenna
ITALY
Tel. 39 0544 451340
Fax. 39 0544 451464
www.sicis.com

SMEDBO AB
P.O. Box 13063
S-250 13 Helsingborg
SWEDEN
Tel. 46 42 251500
Fax. 46 42 251 515
www.smedbo.se

STALLINGA BV
Van Diemenstraat 264
1013 CR Amsterdam
THE NETHERLANDS
Tel. 31 20 4200876
Fax. 31 20 4207037
www.stallinga.nl

STRUCH
Ctra. De Tous, Km. 1
Apdo. Corrreos 12
46260 Alberique
(Valencia)
SPAIN
Tel. 34 963 440 000
Fax. 34 962 441 046
www.struch.es

SUPERGRIF
Pol. Ind. El Plà;
C/ Ramón de Trinchería 1, ap. 50
08980 Sant Feliu de Llobregat
(Barcelona)
SPAIN
Tel. 34 936 859 800
Fax. 34 936 859 810
www.supergrif.com

SYSTEM-POOL
(GRUPO PORCELANOSA)
Ctra. Viver-Pto. Burriana, Km. 63.2
12540 Villarreal
(Castellón)
SPAIN
Tel. 34 964 506 464
Fax. 34 964 506 481
www.system-pool.com

TEUCO GUZZINI SPA
Via Avogadro, 12
Zona Industriale Enrico Fermi
62010 Montelupone (MC)
ITALY
Tel. 39 0733 2201
Fax. 39 0733 220391
www.teuco.it

TEUCO ESPAÑA SL
Pol. Ind. «Can Jardi»
C/ Strauss s/n
08191 Rubí
(Barcelona)
SPAIN
Tel. 34 936 999 162
Fax. 34 935 883 253
www.teuco.es

TOSCOQUATTRO
Via Sila 40
59100 Prato
ITALY
Tel. 39 0574 815535
Fax. 39 0574 815384
www.toscoquattro.it

TREND GROUP
Viale Dell'Industria, 42
36100 Vicenza
ITALY
Tel. 39 0444 23371
Fax. 39 0444 233777
www.trend-vi.com

TREND GROUP
(DISTRIBUTED IN SPAIN BY
MATIMEX)
Pol. Industrial Mijares; C/ Onda,
8-Apdo. 69
12550 Alzamora
(Castellón)
SPAIN
Tel. 34 964 503 240
Fax. 34 964 562 909
www.matimex.es

TRENTINO BAÑO CERÁMICA
Tel. Information for retail outlets:
34 902 152 397
SPAIN
www.trentino.es

TULLI ZUCCARI
Via Faustana, 50 - Borgo Trevi
06032 Trevi (Perugia)
ITALY
Tel. 39 0742 381555
Fax. 39 0742 381636
www.tullizuccari.com

UNITED COLORS OF BENETTON
Benetton Group Spa: Villa Minelli
31050 Ponzano (Treviso)
ITALY
Tel. 39 0422 519111
Fax. 39 0422 969501
www.benetton.com

VALLI & VALLI
L'ARREDOBAGNO
Via Concordia, 16
20055 Renate (Mi)

ITALY
Tel. 39 0362 982258
Fax. 39 0362 999038
www.vallievalli.com

VIELER INTERNATIONAL
Breslauer Straße 34
D-58614 Iserlohn
GERMANY
Tel. 49 02374/52-0
Fax. 49 02374 52268
E-mail: info@vieler.com

VITRAFORM
(CHERRY CREEK GLASS)
3500 Blake Street
80205 Denver, CO
U.S.A.
Tel. 1 303 295 1010
Fax. 1 303 292 1161
www.vitraform.com

VOLA A/S
Lunavej, 2
DK-8700 Horsens
DENMARK
Tel. 45 7023 5500
Fax. 45 7023 5511
www.vola.dk

WET
Via Abetone 18
20137 Milán
ITALY
Tel. 39 02 54123427
Fax. 39 02 54125735
www.wet.co.it

ZUCCHETTI
Via Molini di Resiga 29
28024 Gozzano
(Novara)
ITALY
Tel. 39 0322 954700
Fax. 39 0322 954823
www.zucchetionline.it